After bitter conflict an
water rights, by the 1
is one of the most pea
fornia.

Until its owner, Ysanne de Rivas, returns after spending six months in Monterey to find that the valley is once more filled with tears. Caught up in a feud to gain possession of it, who can she trust? Her only brother Felipe, or Ruy Valdez, the man she believes is responsible for her father's death—the only man she will ever love?

By the same author in Masquerade

FRANCESCA
MADELON
GAMBLER'S PRIZE
A PRIDE OF MACDONALDS
THE COUNTESS
MARIA ELENA
CASTLE OF THE MIST
MOONSHADOW
PRINCE OF DECEPTION
THE SILVER SALAMANDER
WILD WIND IN THE HEATHER

The Valley of Tears
Valentina Luellen

MILLS & BOON LIMITED
London · Sydney · Toronto

*First published in Great Britain 1983
by Mills & Boon Limited, 15–16 Brook's Mews,
London W1A 1DR*

© Valentina Luellen 1983
*Australian copyright 1983
Philippine copyright 1983*

ISBN 0 263 74520 1

The text of this publication or any part thereof may not be reproduced or transmitted in any form or by any means, electronic or mechanical, including photocopying, recording, storage in an information retrieval system, or otherwise, without the written permission of the publisher.

This book is sold subject to the condition that it shall not, by way of trade or otherwise, be lent, resold, hired out or otherwise circulated without the prior consent of the publisher in any form of binding or cover other than that in which it is published and without a similar condition including this condition being imposed on the subsequent purchaser.

Set in 11 on 11½ pt Linotron Times
04/0184

*Photoset by Rowland Phototypesetting Ltd
Bury St Edmunds, Suffolk
Made and printed in Great Britain by
Cox & Wyman Ltd, Reading*

CHAPTER ONE

As THE carriage topped the rise of a hill, Ysanne saw the valley for the first time in six long months and knew she was home, back where she belonged. She made a silent vow never to leave again. She leaned forward in her seat, her eyes scanning the countryside around her as the driver urged the horses down a steep incline.

It had not changed, this long, narrow corridor of land that was hers and hers alone, passed only to the female line of the de Rivas family since the days of her grandmother. It was an area of land ten miles long and two miles wide, flanked on one side by rich grazing land, on the other by sparsely dotted pines which gave way to densely wooded slopes climbing higher, ever higher towards the background of snow-capped mountains. How she loved it. Already she could smell the fragrance of pine trees and notice the difference in the air, so sweet and clear after the odours of Monterey.

The valley was the only access to her father's *hacienda*. Beyond, some twenty miles further north, was the *hacienda* of their nearest neighbour Sancho Morales. Tucked away on the edge of the 'high country', was the *estancia* of her father's dearest friend, Pedro Valdez. The valley was the only direct access to all three properties and therefore of great importance. They were also all totally dependent on the one and only waterhole which lay at the far end of it, on de Rivas land.

In the past it had been the cause of bitter conflict and bloodshed until Ysanne's grandmother, who had first given it the name *Valle de Lágrimas*— Valley of Tears—as she stood over the grave of the husband killed in yet another dispute over access rights, vowed it would never again be owned by a man. In future the women of the de Rivas family would inherit and protect wisely and with foresight, what power-hungry men had fought and killed to possess for years past. And so the right of way was shared, grazing and water rights equally allotted, and peace came to the valley. It was a Valley of Tears no longer.

It seemed incredible, but her prayers had been answered, Ysanne thought. As far as she could see, nothing had changed since the day she went away. Here she had grown up as a child, learned to ride. Here she had laughed and joked and tried her skill against Pedro's two sons and, more often than not, beat the younger one every time. Ruy, the eldest son, had not been so easy to outride . . .

Ruy! She could not say his name even to herself without her heart missing a beat. He must surely have altered in six months. Taller perhaps, stronger, more confident, although confidence was something he had never lacked. He had always been the best at everything, with people, horses, guns and especially women. Tolerating, sometimes only just, the tomboy who rode at his side, constantly challenging his prowess, but never once had he looked at Ysanne the way he looked at other women.

On her nineteenth birthday she had deliberately

flirted with him, determined to make him aware of her more feminine charms, but despite the fact that three sewing maids had worked on her new gown for two weeks, despite the new hairstyle which made her look older, more sophisticated, despite the effort it cost her to act like a lady, he had gone off with another girl after only one dance. She had spent most of the evening discussing horses with his brother, Juan!

That night she made up her mind he would never ignore her again. She loved him. She wanted to be his wife. To achieve that end she knew she would have to employ all the womanly wiles God had so graciously given her. Her decision was a drastic one. She chose self-imposed exile from all those she loved, the house and land she cherished, the father she adored, in a desperate attempt to turn a high-spirited, headstrong girl from an uninteresting duckling to an elegant swan.

In doing so she knew she would be depriving her father of someone he considered more competent to deal with the everyday running of the *hacienda* than the son who preferred wine and horses to work, and had proved a constant disappointment to him since the day he had been thrown from his horse and refused to remount, shaming not only himself with his tears, but the proud father who had given him the stallion for his twelfth birthday.

Ysanne rode like a man and revelled in the knowledge. She commanded the respect of her father's *peónes* because she was willing to work alongside them in times of need, instilling in them fresh vigour with her own tireless efforts. She was her father's right hand, his comforter, advisor as well as a loving daughter. Her departure had been a great loss to him, yet she knew it had also pleased him. A marriage was in the offing if his stubborn daughter had anything to do with it and that meant children—children to inherit what he had built up over the years. Strong-willed, tempestuous, maybe even wild grandchildren if the blood of Ysanne were to mingle with that of the fiery Ruy Valdez!

Poor Papa! Ysanne could still remember that stunned look on his face when she told him she wanted to go away. Then she had explained why and he had taken her in his arms and given her his blessing and immediately begun to talk of the fine grandsons she would give him when she returned to captivate the heart of the man of her choice with the startling transformation. What a union it would be!

'*Momento!*' she cried excitedly and the carriage came to a halt amid a cloud of red-brown dust. She suddenly wanted to climb out and take off her shoes and stockings and feel the earth between her toes as she had done so often as a child. All the months of careful schooling were forgotten, lost in the tumult of emotion which engulfed her.

On the opposite seat her *dueñna*, awakened from her doze, sat up startled and Ysanne hastened to reassure her.

'We are almost home, Serafina. Home at last! How did I endure being away for so long?'

'Don't linger here, *mi niña*. Let us go on.' The woman frowned as she looked around her and recognised their location.

'Go on?' Ysanne echoed. '*Sí*, perhaps we should. Tomorrow I will ride here . . . there is time enough now. Can you imagine the surprise on Papa's face when he sees me? You are sure he suspected nothing when you wanted to stay away overnight?'

'Why should he? He thinks I am visiting my brother. Do not worry, it will be a surprise, little one—for everyone.' There was an oddness in Serafina's tone that Ysanne, in her joy to be back, failed to notice. She took her companion's frequent glances through the window as confirmation she too was glad her mistress had returned to surroundings she loved.

'How do I look?' Ysanne entreated. She felt hot and flushed from the journey. She wanted to look her best for her father. Him first and then later . . .

'Beautiful, as always.'

'Not—as always. More beautiful than when I went away? More grown up? A lady?' Ysanne suggested.

Serafina, above all people, could be relied upon to tell her the truth. Dear, plump old Serafina, who had raised her from the cradle, outlived three husbands, but never produced children of her own and so had lavished on Ysanne enough love for a dozen. She was both friend and mother when the occasion demanded, fierce protector of the mistress she adored. There was nothing the woman would not do for her.

'You have come home a fine lady. Your father will be proud to receive you back beneath his roof. As for the other one . . .' Serafina paused, watching Ysanne's cheeks colour slightly. She knew she should have said before the journey began—'stay in Monterey, my little innocent. Find a handsome *caballero* who will steal your heart and erase the foolish infatuation you feel for this other one. Things were not as they were before you went away, everything has changed. The valley is once more tearful . . .' These were the words she should have spoken before it was too late. The fault had been hers. Her task was now to protect her mistress through whatever lay ahead . . . protect at all costs, and so she forced a smile to her stiff lips and shrugged broad shoulders. 'If he does not notice you now he is blind and not worthy of the sacrifice you have made.'

'Has he come often to the house?' Ysanne asked, a catch in her voice. 'Has he spoken of me—asked how I am? When I am coming home?'

'For that you will have to ask Don Diego, your father. I do not listen at keyholes,' Serafina returned and this time Ysanne looked across at her curiously.

Her *duenña* was and always had been a notorious gossip. Her tongue was never still. Yet now she remained silent!

Dear God, she thought, he has found someone else! Perhaps taken a wife! She opened her mouth to ask, then closed it firmly again. Another few miles and she would be home and her father would gladly answer all her questions.

She instructed the driver to continue and sat back in her seat, smoothing out the creases in her skirts produced by the long hours of sitting, first in the overland coach from Monterey, then in the tiny carriage which had been waiting, together with Serafina, to transport her home from the way station where she had stayed overnight.

Six months in Monterey, in the house of strict Tía Dolores, a widow who had had much experience in the grooming of her own five daughters, had changed her. Where before she would have been unable to contain the questions mounting inside her, she now remained quiet, a demure expression on her face. She had learned patience—and so much more. Pretty dresses and afternoon tea under the watchful eye of a sour *duenña*, incapable of smiling, had replaced boyish work clothes and long rides into the mountains, to lie beneath the sweet-smelling pines and dream the dreams she dared tell no one but Serafina.

Polite conversation instead of jokes and laughter with Ruy and Juan or loyal old Pablo, the head groom who had taught her to ride when she was five years old. Evenings spent at the opera instructing her mind, instead of in front of the huge open fire in the *sala* with her beloved father. Lessons on how to be a good hostess in her own home, how to receive guests and plan every day down to the last detail, however trivial it might seem. Long, boring lessons, day after day, month after month. How to walk, smile, listen when she was bursting with questions. How to satisfy the whims of her husband, never forgetting for one moment he would always be her master and she must walk forever in his shadow. Ysanne's comments on that had earned her the sharpest end of Tía Dolores tongue. She had accepted the rebuke in a meek silence and made no further comment, without allowing one word of what was being said to sink into her. No one, not even the man she loved, was going to turn her into a mindless cabbage!

Even Tía Dolores, critical to the last, was forced to admit that Ysanne was a good and eager pupil and, after six short months, ready to return home. In her usual dour tone, she commented that Ysanne would now make some *caballero* an obedient and faithful wife, the mother of many fine sons.

Not any man—just one! The man whose cool

mockery of many years had at last penetrated her outward show of indifference. Outwardly? Yes, she had changed, but deep inside her the same fires still raged and could only be quenched by the love of the man for whom this conversion had been affected. How could he not fail to notice her now?

Tonight she would share her homecoming with her father and her brother, Felipe, but tomorrow . . . She would ride to the Valdez *estancia*. No! That was too obvious. A party to welcome her home— yes, that was a better idea and she would invite all her friends. There would be no way that Ruy Valdez could know he would be top of the list. She would be gay and charming and witty . . . and pray every moment that his dark eyes would hold interest as they looked at her. They must! She had gone too far to turn back now. Nothing, but nothing was going to stop her from marrying him, no matter how long it took, whatever obstacles she had to overcome. She would love him forever.

The carriage came to a halt so abruptly she was flung from her seat on top of Serafina and for a moment she could only lie breathless against the huge bosom, her senses reeling.

The sound of angry voices came from outside. As Ysanne roused herself, the door was wrenched open and a face, caked with blood and dirt, appeared. Serafina screamed and crossed herself, declaring they were about to be robbed and murdered.

Robbed! Here, on her land! No one would dare! The momentary fear Ysanne experienced was thrust to one side in anger. As a grubby hand coupled her wrist, trying to pull her bodily from the carriage, she grabbed a leather overnight case from the seat and aimed it at the man's head. With a grunt of pain he released her and fell back onto the ground.

'No! No, *mi niña*, you don't know what you are doing,' Serafina cried as she began to climb down, her eyes as hard and angry as two brilliant emeralds. 'We must drive on.'

Ysanne did not answer. Words were beyond her at the sight which befell her eyes.

A few hundred yards away were the first of the dwellings belonging to one of the four villages which lined the valley floor. Here lived many of her father's *peónes* who daily tilled the corn and wheat fields, and watched over his horses and cattle as they grazed on the rich pastureland. She knew the men and women who lived here. Many came to the *hacienda* each year after the crops had been harvested, an annual occasion when Don Diego showed his gratitude for all their hard work by arranging three days of festivities. In times of hardship he always ensured they had enough food for their stomachs, wood for their fires. He fed them, clothed them, gave them roofs over their heads. He was a benevolent employer—had many not said so to his face?

She leaned back against the carriage, uncaring that the beautiful new gown she had bought especially for the trip was streaked with dust. Inches of dust already covered her shoes, but she did not notice that either. Her eyes were riveted on the scene before her. Only one house still stood, with fire raging within its walls, consuming what little roof was left. Even as she watched, horrified, the last of it fell and was consumed in the fierce flames. The rest of the buildings were gutted, smouldering ruins. Chickens and other animals lay slaughtered all around her. In a pathetic huddle, men, women and children stared across at her, sullen-eyed. Many of them were bruised and bleeding. One lay inert on the ground before the crowd. The shirt had been torn from his back and he had been viciously beaten until there was nothing but a mass of bloody red weals.

'In God's name, what has happened here?' Ysanne cried.

'Who are you to call on God?' a hate-filled voice rasped out from one man.

'You know me. I am Ysanne de Rivas, the daughter of Don Diego.' They were not blind, of course they recognised her. She had not been away that long and, now she had been staring at them for some while, she could remember many of the hostile faces. Never before had she seen such hatred in the eyes which watched her.

'We know you—Doña Ysanne.' A young woman stepped forward, dishevelled, bleeding from a cut on her mouth.

'María Teresa!' Ysanne exclaimed in relief. For a moment some of those eyes were beginning to unnerve her. Murderous, was the only description for what she saw in them. But María Teresa had served as a maid in the *hacienda*, leaving, only a few weeks before Ysanne herself departed, to marry a local boy. She had been at their wedding and drank their health. 'Tell me what has happened. Who has dared to do this to you?'

To her horror and growing alarm, the woman threw back her head and burst into laughter . . . shrill laughter which bordered on hysteria. What had she stumbled on here? Her brain refused to function under the shock of what she had come upon. Not since the early days when her mother had been in possession of the valley had anyone dared violate its inhabitants, who had lived in peace for the first time in their lives. For the first time since the Valle de Lágrimas was given its name.

'I am waiting for an answer,' Ysanne declared in a calm, clear voice, which betrayed none of the apprehension mounting inside her. Once these people had been trusted employees, content and, in their own way, prosperous. Now the enmity radiating from each and every one of them told her that had all ended. They looked at her as if they hated her, but why should they? She had done nothing—she had been away!

'The fine lady wants an answer,' someone called out jeeringly.

'An answer she shall have. Look, Ysanne de Rivas, do you see this man who lies at my feet? Do you know whose blood soaks my skirts? That of my husband—the father of my child not yet born.' Mará Teresa advanced to where Ysanne stood, and spat full in her face. 'May you and your family rot in the fires of hell. This was done on the orders of Don Diego himself.'

With a cry of rage Serafina flung herself from the carriage and slapped the woman to the ground, then placed her huge body between her mistress and the menacing figures which stepped forward, hands outstretched to grasp her.

'Don't you dare lay a finger on her, any of you. Have you all gone mad?' She screamed the words at them, but they fell on deaf ears. Two of the strongest men grabbed hold of her and unceremoniously threw her into the arms of the waiting crowd. She was forced to the ground and sat on to keep her there. That accomplished, all attention was turned on Ysanne.

'Send her back to Don Diego the same way as my Roberto has been left here with me,' María Teresa cried. 'An eye for an eye . . .'

Someone grabbed up a large branch of wood from the ground. Another seized a broom salvaged from the fires. Several men began to take off their belts as they advanced towards the slender figure trapped against the side of the carriage.

'Beat me . . . you would not dare lay hands on me . . .' Ysanne could not believe this was really happening.

She screamed in terror as she was seized from both sides and dragged forward. She heard a tearing sound as a woman from behind fastened her fingers in her dress and ripped it from neck to waist. Strong and supple though her body was, six months of inactivity in Monterey had weakened her. She kicked out at the men trying to force her to the ground, as she would have done before had anyone dared to lay indecent hands on her, but then she would have been wearing close-fitting trousers and knee-length boots which could do some damage, not heavy skirts and dainty leather shoes with silver buckles which caught in the material of her gown and sent her pitching to her knees.

'Now! Now!' she could hear María Teresa pleading.

Ysanne tried to speak but there was dirt in her mouth. She gathered the last of her strength to attempt to rise, to face these half-crazed people and find the words to instill in them some sense of sanity, but her loose hair was wound around someone's fist and her head was jerked forward again towards the hard earth. Her cry of pain evoked laughter which chilled her to the bone. She had never known such fear in all her young life.

The laughter and voices became muffled in her ears as a great blackness threatened to descend upon her, offering blessed relief from the pain and humiliation about to be forced on her.

Voices . . . different voices penetrated her dimming senses. The sound of horses hoofs drumming over the ground. Her arms were suddenly freed, the agonising hold on her hair relaxed. Weakly she lifted her head, saw through a blur of tears that her attackers were falling back from her. Those that did not were herded away by mounted horsemen.

She sat back on her heels, rubbing bruised wrists, staring unbelievingly at the tall figure who flung himself from his horse and ran to her side. At first she had thought the riders belonged to her father's *hacienda*, but no, the face which came close to hers, the arms which gently supported her, lifted her to her feet, held her for a long moment as she buried her face against a solid shoulder shaking with relief, belonged to the very same man who haunted her thoughts day and night. The man who had invaded her dreams during those six long months absence. How cruel fate was that they should meet in this manner!

'Ruy!' His name was a whisper on her lips. Of all men he had been the one to save her!

A fierce expletive exploded under the man's breath. Reaching out he smoothed back the loose hair which partially hid her face and it was not until that moment she realised he had not known who she was.

'Ysanne! *Dios*—you!' The disbelief in his tone

equalled hers. She was held at arms' length and swept from head to toe with eyes that were as black as jet. They narrowed in anger at the sight of her torn gown, the dirt which streaked her cheeks, the bruises already beginning to show against the creamy whiteness of her skin. 'They will pay for every mark . . .'

'I—I am—not hurt . . . just frightened. They were going to beat me. In heaven's name why?'

She could no longer contain her tears and they burst forth in an uncontrollable flood. It was several minutes before she was able to compose herself again. He continued to hold her in silence, his gaze never leaving her ashen face.

'Get her into the carriage and keep her there,' he ordered, handing her into Serafina's comforting embrace.

'Ruy, what is happening?' His harsh tone made Ysanne feel uneasy—and the fact that he turned on his heel and left her as if he had not heard her question.

He strode purposefully across to the two men who had been holding her when he rode up, and Ysanne watched his open palm strike first one and then the other. She heard the fury in the words tossed at them.

'You fools! She is innocent of what has happened. Have you forgotten she has been away?'

'She is of his blood,' one of the men whined.

'Idiot! Animal!' His words only served to increase the anger of Ruy Valdez, and the next blow he received felled him to the ground. He lay there, too frightened to move, staring up at six feet of solid muscle and bone and silently pleading for mercy.

Ysanne knew Ruy to be a man of unpredictable moods which could go from terrible anger to contrition, gentleness to passion, in the space of a heartbeat. It was one of the things she liked about him—the human weakness of vulnerability. So strong, yet fallible. From one day to the next she never knew how it would be when they met. It was exciting more often than frustrating, but never before had she seen him come so close to completely losing control.

'Get into the carriage, *mi niña*.' Serafina tried unsuccessfully to make Ysanne do as she had been told, but the girl stubbornly shook her head. The villagers were being lifted on to horses. Those able to walk followed the cavalcade which slowly began to move off under the watchful eyes of Ruy Valdez.

Now that she was safe and the fear of what might have happened was receding she was again plagued by questions as to why she had been so cruelly manhandled and why the village had been razed to the ground, livestock needlessly slaughtered, a man killed in the most barbaric fashion.

This was her land. How dared anyone violate something so sacred! There should have been men from the *hacienda* to combat such lawlessness, but then the words María Teresa had spoken returned to haunt her. 'This was done on the orders of Don Diego himself.' Never! Her father was not a butcher, he had no reason to order the destruction of one of his own villages and its inhabitants. People who had been born in the valley, farmed it, built their homes and reared their families on the lush grazing land bordering it. All under his protection!

This was the Year of Our Lord 1847, and California was no longer the savage land it had been when the Spaniards first set foot on it, or the monks following in their footsteps built their first church and opened its doors to the poor heathen *Indios* who wandered the land. Under Mexican rule, it had flourished, although the constant changes of government and often lawless rule of the army had now brought dissension to the country. But it had never touched the valley or the town. Nothing ever changed here.

Yet there had been no mistake. Don Diego, she had said, with hatred in her eyes and in her voice. Once she had called him her father, for her own had been killed when she was only three years old. He had brought both María Teresa and her mother into his employ and when the latter died, had cared for the daughter until the day he gave her away in marriage. On that day he had allocated bride and bridegroom several hectares of land below the rich timber country which lay behind the village. Good, fertile land where they could live in peace and raise a family—and with hard work, prosper. On that day too, María Teresa had called Diego de Rivas her father. What terrible thing had happened that she now disowned him, demanded vengeance, cursed his name and had no friendship for the daughter with whom she had grown up.

Serafina knew, Ysanne thought, looking into the closed face of the woman at her side and realising how silent the insatiable chatterbox had been throughout the whole journey. In her excitement she had not realised how silent, how evasive she had been when questions had been asked in rapid succession. What had she come home to?

Ruy stood for a long time after the cavalcade of

horsemen, many carrying children in front of them, moved away. Men and women followed in a sullen silence, carrying whatever remnants they had managed to salvage from their burning homes. They trusted him, yet they cursed her father! They should have turned to her in their need.

Slowly he turned and walked back to her. The expression on the sunburnt features was bitter.

'Is someone going to tell me what is going on?' Her tone was sharp with frustration. 'Where are you taking those people? They are my father's *peónes*.'

'They are being taken to a place of safety. I gave them the choice of confronting Don Diego with their accusations or going with my men. Their choice was a simple one. They no longer have confidence in him. They prefer to trust me. This is not the first time villages in the valley have been put to the torch. The last time was less than three weeks ago.'

'Impossible. They are protected,' Ysanne stormed, her temper rising.

'Protected? By whom? You, Ysanne, from Monterey? In six whole months you did not return once to ask after the people you profess to care for. Your father then? He is old and not in good health. That leaves only Felipe . . .'

'What did you say?' Ysanne's fingers, clutching at the torn gown about her shoulders, whitened visibly. 'What are you saying? I have corresponded with my father every month. Not once has he mentioned his health is failing. What has he kept from me? What are you keeping from me?'

'Get into the carriage, Ysanne. We will talk on the way to the *hacienda*.' Ruy said with a frown.

'And we will have to do something about your state of undress, if your arrival is not to cause a sensation.'

'Are you concerned for your reputation, my dear Ruy? You once told me you were not interested in this scarecrow of a tomboy.'

'Times change, as you will soon discover. I take it this homecoming is meant to be a surprise?'

'*Sí*. I hope my father and brother are more pleased to see me than you appear to be. If you will kindly ask Sebastián to hand down the large chest up there on the carriage and leave us for a while, I will ensure my appearance causes you no further embarrassment.'

'You haven't changed. Still a little spit-fire underneath all those fine silks and frills. Now you are back we might be able to get to the bottom of this conflict,' came the dry retort as he received the heavy trunk from the coachman and set it down on the ground before her.

'Find me something to wear, Serafina. Anything,' she said, hurriedly climbing inside and pulling down the window blinds to shield her from Ruy's gaze. Not that it proved necessary, she found, for he had already turned his back on her and was wandering slowly towards the gutted houses, where he began an inspection of each and every one—as far as it was possible.

She had been changed and waiting for some ten minutes before he returned. She had chosen a dress of pale blue silk out of the two Serafina produced, quite demure in its simplicity. Wait until he saw the gown she had had made for her homecoming party, she mused, as he lowered himself into the opposite seat and crossed one dusty booted leg over the other, appraising her appearance in silence for a long moment.

She had lost a good deal of weight during the time she had been away and the tomboy figure he was accustomed to seeing in tight-fitting hide breeches and a shirt, was now displayed to advantage inside one of the latest styles from Paris, which accentuated young, full breasts and a tiny waist.

His eyes lingered on the red-gold crown of curls swept high on to the top of her head by Serafina's deft fingers, and the green eyes, as brilliant as emeralds, framed by dark lashes, before moving down over her body to complete his inspection and bring a flush of embarrassed colour to her already pink cheeks. Before she went away she would have returned stare for stare, challenge for challenge, but it had been six long months since she had last looked into those dark, smouldering eyes.

Many men had admired her during that time. Some had wanted to do more than just look, but none of them had ever made her so aware of herself as Ruy Valdez was doing at this moment.

At last he was seeing her as she had prayed he would—a woman! Not a tousle-headed child, his equal on a horse but never on the dance floor. A companion capable of enjoying a joke, returning a mocking taunt, but never his choice to accompany him on social occasions.

Her triumphant moment did not last. She became aware his thoughts were drifting away from her as he turned to look out of the window. Something more important than her took precedence in his mind, she realised as he called up to Sebastián to drive on.

'How is everyone at home?' she asked in an

effort to force her mind over the traumatic experience she had just undergone. She knew by the fierce ache in her arms and shoulders that they would be covered in bruises by the morning. A few words of sympathy from Ruy would have comforted her.

'You have come back in time for a wedding.' There was an oddness in his tone which made her look at him closely, but his expression told her nothing and she put it down to imagination. Her frayed nerves were playing tricks. 'Juan is to marry Manuela.'

Manuela was the ward of Pedro Valdez, the daughter of an old friend, whom he had taken into his home when she became parentless. Ysanne wondered how her brother had received the news. From the very first day he had seen Manuela, he had professed to love her, yet her father had never mentioned it, to her knowledge, when Pedro made one of his many visits to their *hacienda*.

'Manuela spoke of her wish that you be asked to be one of her bridesmaids,' Ruy continued, 'but I told her you would not consider it worthwhile returning home for such a small occasion. It seems fate has brought you anyway.'

'Then you took too much upon yourself. Of course I would have come, had I been informed. Could you not have taken the trouble to write and tell me?'

'As a matter of fact I came to Monterey to see you. I was received by that dragon of an aunt who told me you were at the theatre with friends and would not be returning until late. I said I would call again in the morning. Her reply indicated I would not be welcome. "Don Diego has placed her in my care to train her for marriage and that I have done", I can still remember her words so clearly.' The eyes intent on Ysanne's startled features were full of mockery, as if he found the thought of her as a wife and mother profoundly amusing! '"I have already conveyed to him my satisfaction at her progress. The man of his choice will have no cause to be dissatisfied with her."'

'She—she said that!' she gasped in horror. 'She had no right.'

'She thought she had. She obviously considered me an unsuitable companion for the new Ysanne,' came the infuriating reply. He was laughing at her!

'Why should I not think of marriage?' she demanded. 'I shall soon be twenty. Most of my friends are already settled with a husband and family.'

'A truly great age,' Ruy teased, and chuckled as two fierce spots of colour began to burn on her cheeks. 'I can give you ten years and I have not committed myself yet. Why should I, when I already have everything I want?'

Then I shall have to change your mind, Ysanne thought, undaunted by his words.

'I am going to have a party for my homecoming. It will give me a chance to see everyone again and perhaps someone will have some ideas on who is behind these attacks in the valley. Someone must know something! Will you come and bring Juan and Manuela? Then I can tell her myself how pleased I shall be to be one of her bridesmaids.' Her tone chided him once again for his high-handedness over the matter. Too busy to attend, indeed! She was most unladylike in her thoughts of Tía Dolores. How dare she send Ruy away! She had said nothing of his visit, given no hint of how close Ysanne had come to seeing the man she loved. What must he have thought? He now knew why she had gone away—or at least, half the reason. She would wipe that sardonic smile from his face very soon.

She would dazzle him in her elegant gown. In her role as hostess she would show him how the 'scraggy urchin' had been tamed, on the surface at least. She intended to make it quite clear to everyone who Ysanne Margarita Lucía de Rivas had chosen as her husband.

They were passing the side road which led towards his home. The sunbaked, well-ridden track snaked over sloping hills where it was perpetual spring, through varied orchards of fruit trees. Up into the grassy, wooded slopes where herds of deer grazed beneath the sharp eyes of birds of prey. Where wild geese and ducks refreshed themselves in crystal clear mountain streams and the wolves howled their solitary sonatas at night. Up and up, to disappear into the multi-specied firs and pines which dominated the approach to the Sierras.

'Don't you think your father would like to be consulted first?'

'He will agree. By the sound of it he needs something to cheer him up. Why didn't he tell me he was in ill health?' she asked with a frown.

'Perhaps he thought it best not to worry you while you were being groomed for this mammoth transformation. I must admit, on the surface, it appears to have worked. I only hope you will think it all worthwhile now you are home again, or will you not be staying long?'

'You are evading my question, Ruy. That is not like you.'

So many unanswered questions. Her father's

deteriorating health, the burnt village and the hatred of the people who had once been their friends. How many more problems did she know nothing about?

She felt a light touch on her arm and looked into Serafina's smiling face. Was it relief she saw there?

'We are almost home. Look, *mi niña*!'

Home! She had dreamt of this moment for six long months. They were now at the cut-off which led to the Hacienda de las Flores. The House of Flowers. Her father had given it that name in honour of the gardens she had painstakingly created and taken part in constructing herself, around the low, Spanish-style house. Roses bloomed most of the year, succulents in profusion. There were small flowering shrubs bordering the long walkways to the outside walls, hibiscus trees with their scarlet flowers shown off to perfection against the background of white. She had placed hanging baskets on the patio where she loved to eat first thing in the morning and in the cool of the evening with her beloved father and brother. There was a small orchard containing peach, orange and pear trees, with large juicy melons growing in neat rows between.

Rich purple bougainvillaea cascaded over the wrought-iron balustrades encircling the first floor, alongside scarlet poinsettias. It was a riot of colour, as beautiful as when she went away.

La Hacienda de las Flores. She was home!

CHAPTER TWO

To HER immense relief, Ysanne could find nothing changed in the scene which met her eyes. She thought, as the carriage rolled through the main gates, that the whole place looked as if it had been freshly painted. Everything was so brilliantly white in the sunlight, she had to shield her eyes against the glare as Ruy helped her to alight. She stood for a long moment in silence, appreciating what she had come back to. Had she not been so confident that her father was ignorant of her arrival, she would have suspected special preparations had been in progress for her homecoming.

The flower beds were perfect—not a single weed. Several *peónes* were still working on the long path which led around the back of the house to the orchard which was her pride and joy. The trees would be in blossom now, preparing for the summer crop. It was a good time to come back. The grapevine entwined over the lower verandah had begun to produce new leaves and the faithful old bougainvillaea outside her bedroom window still bloomed in a mass of purple.

There was an addition to the stables, she noticed. In the excitement of seeing her father again, she must not forget to look in on the three-year-old chestnut stallion she had left behind. Had he missed her as much as she had him and the daily rides they took together into the foothills of the Sierras? Or in the sweet-smelling pine forests which stretched for miles below them?

A smile touched her lips as she drew a deep breath and at once caught the aroma of freshly baked bread. The kitchen would be in a turmoil, with the Mexican woman who ruled it with an iron hand supervising the making of bread and cakes as she did every morning. Ysanne hoped she had returned on a day when there would be pancakes soaked in honey which was Rosa's speciality and her own particular favourite.

So many different sounds filled the air about her. The heavy thudding of a hammer as it struck the anvil in the smithy's forge, almost drowning the soft singing of women sitting in the shade of some trees grinding corn. Children calling to each other as they ran across the square within the enclosure, carefree and happy, not needing constant supervision from their parents who knew the high walls encircling the *hacienda* protected them from all harm. On the roof above her head, white fan-tail doves cooed softly as they preened themselves.

'Oh, Ruy, I am so glad to be home. I shall never leave again,' she whispered and her voice broke under the strain of emotion which momentarily engulfed her.

He was still holding her hand. He had not released it after she stepped down from the carriage. He raised it to his lips and gently touched the slender fingers.

'Welcome home, Ysanne. There are many watching us now who will thank God for your return, believe me.'

'I have no idea what you mean. If you are in some way insinuating that my return may stop whatever trouble there is in the valley, then I only wish I had come sooner.'

'Your being home again will mean nothing unless you really intend to stay.'

Again she sensed underlying tension in his voice. He was no longer at ease in her company and that troubled her.

'I do.' She stared at him, puzzled and more than a little angry that he had so abruptly spoiled her pleasant moment.

'What of this prospective husband?' The black eyebrows rose quizzingly.

'Married—or single, the valley remains in my possession until I pass it on to my daughter or my closest living relative,' she retorted. 'Six months I am away and by the look of it, you are already at each other's throats. Men! Always you must have the power.'

'I hope I am not included in that statement,' Ruy challenged and a grim expression settled over his handsome features.

'As you told me less than an hour ago, times change. People change too, don't they?'

'I am beginning to realise if anyone has changed, it is you! When you left we were friends. You would never have dreamed of tossing such an accusation at me. One thing I have never coveted is power. I thought you knew me better.'

'A friend would not have turned around and left Monterey without seeing me. You would have found a way to tell me my father was ill and needed me. Tell me of the trouble here. I would have come back with you without hesitation.'

'I wonder.' His tone was noncommittal and she pursed her lips angrily.

'Do not presume to know my mind, Ruy.'

'I stayed on in Monterey for two days,' he said and her eyes widened in surprise. 'I saw you riding in the park, surrounded by a bevy of young *caballeros*, who your aunt obviously considered worthy of your company, because she was dozing on a seat near the entrance. I followed you to the theatre too, but I left early. The woman I watched in velvet and silk, enjoying every moment of the attention being pressed upon her, belonged in Monterey—not the Hacienda de las Flores.'

Ysanne gasped at the insult. Acting instinctively, she slapped him across one cheek. How could he be so blind? Had she endured those months away from him, from everything she loved, only to hear herself condemned for enjoying herself? Those times had been few and far between. Of course she had enjoyed a little flattery, what woman did not? She had been secure in the knowledge that not one of the young men would succeed in turning her head. Her heart was pledged to another, the man now looking at her with contempt in his eyes as he stepped back; said stiffly,

'My horse has a loose shoe. I suggest you go in and greet your father while I have it seen to. I will join you later. Perhaps by then we shall both have cooled a little. Please make my apologies to Don Diego for my absence.'

Without answering, Ysanne picked up her skirts and mounted the stairs to the verandah. She was too furious for explanations, which he might very well have taken for excuses anyway. She had no need to excuse her behaviour!

'Take no notice of him, *mi niña*. He is a blind fool. Anyone can see you have not changed,' Serafina said, hurrying after her.

Ysanne paused to look back at the tall figure leading his horse towards the forge, then her eyes became fixed on the face of her companion.

'You have some questions to answer. When I have seen my father and brother you will tell me what I want to know. Go upstairs and have my trunk unpacked—and wait for me.' Her tone belied argument.

'Don Diego will be in his study. Since his illness he always likes to rest for at least an hour before lunch,' Serafina replied before walking away.

Reproach in her tone too! Dear heaven, what had been happening in the short time she had been away? Her high-heeled leather shoes tapped out a loud warning of her approach on the polished tiles as she crossed the entrance hall, piled high with potted plants and succulents, and entered the cool interior of the house. She had dreamed of this coolness during those days in the house of Tía Dolores, where the doors and windows were always tightly shut, the rooms dark and airless; suffocating.

Great thought had been given to the building of the Hacienda de las Flores by her grandfather. Constructed of stone, in places four feet thick, it was warm in winter, cool in the torrid, dry heat of summer. Every window throughout the house had a pair of stout shutters outside, protection once upon a time against *bandidos* and *indios* who roamed the country, and a pair inside. At any given time the windows could be opened, with the inside slatted pine blinds giving the necessary controlled ventilation without allowing in the overwhelming heat.

The sunlight stealing its way through the shutters now on to the floor at her feet reminded Ysanne of Pinos Altos, the Valdez house. The magnificent structure had been built from giant redwood trees, brought overland from the coast by Pedro Valdez. The interior, every hallway, room and crevice, was panelled in pine, in varying degrees of colour. It lacked the touch of a woman, she remembered, for Ruy's mother had died a few hours after giving birth to her second son and the two boys had been raised by a Navajo woman.

Pausing before a mirror, she scrutinised her appearance. After what had befallen her she looked remarkably calm. The strict indoctrination from Tía Dolores to compose herself when the temper accompanying her red hair threatened to break loose, had won through. She was angry, but it did not show in the serene features. Excited, yet the flush of colour in her cheeks was not unbecoming. Her mind reeled with questions, but she thrust them aside as she opened the study door. Why was it, she wondered, that she longed for those carefree days past when none of these restrictions would have mattered to her. If she was angry, she would have shown it! Her aunt had drained her of all her natural exuberance, she realised, yet unbidden it had returned the moment she stepped over the threshold of her home again.

'And, why, may I ask, has my daughter been talking with everyone but the father waiting to greet her for the last ten minutes?' a voice reprimanded, not unkindly, off to her left.

She spun around with a soft gasp, then, forgetful

of all those important lessons, flung herself into the outstretched arms waiting to receive her.

'Papa! I am so thoughtless. I did not mean to linger.' She smothered the lined face with kisses. He smelt, as always, of his favourite pipe tobacco.

Tonight she would fill it for him and sit on a cushion at his feet in the *sala* as in the days before she went away. Her vision was so blurred with tears she could hardly see his face and, with a sob, she buried her cheek against his shoulder.

'Welcome home, Ysanne,' Diego de Rivas said quietly. Ruy's words, but now full of tenderness, love! 'Welcome back, my daughter.'

'I should not have gone away,' she sobbed. Ruy's words had deeply wounded her, shattering the wonderful dream she had nurtured during her absence and brought back hoping it would become reality. 'Why did you not let me know you were ill? Of this trouble in the Valle de Lágrimas?'

Diego held his daughter at arms' length and stared long and hard into the tear-streaked face. He had aged five years in the time she had been away, Ysanne thought in growing alarm. His hair was almost totally white now. His eyes were ringed with grey shadows of illness and his skin had an unhealthy pallor to it which she had never seen before. So much so quickly! And she had not been at his side to offer comfort and assistance.

'I have failed you,' she said brokenly and her words brought a fierce expletive from Diego's lips.

'That you could never do. Did you not take the place of the son who dishonoured me? Have you not been my right hand these past years?'

'Papa, you promised never to speak of Felipe like that again,' she protested.

'Then do not talk to me of failure. When you are the wife of Ruy Valdez you will be content. I will be content and I will have many fine grandchildren to bounce on my knees before I depart this world. You have always given me everything, my dearest child. Every ounce of your time, your love, even when it deprived you of many things a young girl should have been given by her father. This time you shall have your heart's desire, whatever the cost. You shall have the man you have chosen, I promise. It is a pity my friend Pedro will not be able to see the union of his son and my daughter.'

'What is wrong?' Ysanne asked. 'Is he ill? Not . . .'

Diego nodded, his eyes filled with sadness. So that was why Ruy had sounded so odd and had never mentioned his father. It had not been her imagination after all. Such a friendship Diego and Pedro had shared, as close as brothers might have been. Once or twice a week they would visit each others' homes, stay to dinner and chat long into the early hours. Their conversations fascinated Ysanne, for she learned of the early days when they had first come together. The difficulties when the Hacienda de las Flores was built by her grandfather, of the life in a new and strange country, with little or no contact with anyone speaking their native Spanish, except for a few priests who ran the sparsely dotted missions.

Of how Pedro Valdez had built Pinos Altos, often working alongside the men, mostly *indios* from the nearest mission, together with a few provided by her father, so that the house would be finished quickly and he could bring his bride of a few months from Spain to join him. Side by side, from the first day, they met with never a cross word between them.

'An accident about two months ago, after a visit here. We had talked the night away. You know how it was between us, with much drinking and reminiscing. The next morning Ruy discovered his father's bed had not been slept in and thinking he had stayed here the night, he rode over. Instead he found him dead, thrown from his horse. *Dios mío*, such injuries to his poor head. He must have died instantly.'

Tenderly he wiped the tears from both their eyes, said with a smile, that eased the tension from his face,

'Is he not still a *muy guápo hombre*, this Ruy?'

'Very handsome,' Ysanne admitted.

'Still the same one you wish to spend the rest of your life with?'

'The same . . . but . . .' How could she explain the strangeness between them now. She did not even understand it herself.

'No buts, my child. I have several reasons for inviting him here today, the prime one being the proposed match between you. I had no idea you would return so quickly after receiving my letter. This was meant to be a surprise.'

'Letter?' Ysanne echoed. 'Papa, I have not heard from you in over three weeks. I was lonely and homesick for the *hacienda*. *Sí*, missing Ruy too. I could not stay a moment longer in Monterey.'

'You must have left before it arrived. No matter. You are here and we are together again.'

'I will never go away again. I promise.'

'I hope not. I am looking forward to seeing you well and truly settled within the next few months.

Let me look at you. *Dios!* So grown up now. Such a lady.'

'I have not really changed. Not inside.'

'Sufficiently, I think, to attract his attention,' Diego laughed softly. 'Come and sit down. I'll have Juanita bring us something cool to drink. Ruy will be joining us soon, I hope?'

'In a little while. His horse has a loose shoe. Papa, before he comes, we must talk.' Ysanne waited until they had been served with glasses of ice-cold orange juice before she said, 'On the way here I saw the village of some of our *peónes* devastated. A man had been killed! Ruy spoke of this happening before. I felt great anger in him; frustration. He spoke as if he thought I had turned my back on my responsibilities and gone away to enjoy myself and I could not tell him otherwise. Not yet. I have to know what is happening.'

'There is little to tell. I try not to think of who may be responsible. It would be so easy to place the blame.'

'Would it? Do you know who is responsible for these outrages? The men responsible must be punished. One of the women accused you personally of being to blame, but I know that cannot be possible.'

'I have asked myself many times what could be behind these attacks, these attempts as I see them to clear the Valle de Lágrimas of people and livestock, and turn it back to what it used to be in your grandmother's time, nothing but a right of way.'

'When grandfather used to exact a toll for anyone wanting to use it. It was useless land then. Nothing grew there. It was an access only, with the waterhole at the far end. He made himself rich with ths money he was given to lease it out to tenant farmers and was killed by some poor men he pushed too far. Since then the valley has prospered, hasn't it? We have all lived in peace with one another.'

'Perhaps someone has grown ambitious over the years and seeks the power that ownership of the valley could give him.'

'I own it. No one can take that away from me.'

'Unless you were not here. Perhaps your absence made them believe you had gone for good. I told no one the real reason, not even Felipe.'

'Papa, there are so few people who could benefit from owning the valley. Two people at the most. Felipe, my own brother—or . . .'

Diego nodded gravely as her voice lapsed into an awkward silence.

'Ruy. That is why I place no blame. My own son or the man who is to become my son-in-law.'

'Felipe has no need of the valley. I am his sister and if, as you say, he has no knowledge of why I went away, then he has no reason to believe anything has changed!' Felipe, her brother, capable of inflicting such destruction, causing the death of a human being in such a barbaric fashion? She would never believe it. He had always been a fragile child, shy and insecure, hating violence of any kind. The sight of blood had once made him faint, much to their father's disgust.

He had always been her mother's favourite, she remembered. Over the years Ysanne had found herself slipping easily into the place he had vacated at her father's side, eager for his company, his knowledge and never minding the fact he came to regard her more and more as a son instead of a daughter.

'Who has been looking after everything while you were ill?' she asked.

'Since my illness, trouble with my heart Dr Sanchez tells me, Felipe has done so. For a few weeks we were closer than we had been for years, but soon his impatience with the *vaqueros*, his lack of interest in anything of importance began to cause friction between us. You know, of course, of his infatuation for Manuela?' When Ysanne nodded, her father settled himself back into his chair, his features growing solemn. 'About two months after you left he spoke of wishing to marry her. Here in this very room, while Pedro was here, without having the good manners to consult me first. Manuela had already made plain to Pedro the feelings she has for Juan. He and I both agreed a match with Felipe was out of the question under the circumstances. My son disgraced himself yet again, falling into such a rage I thought he had taken leave of his senses. He cursed the pair of us before storming out of the room. Naturally Pedro and I were upset, concerned, but as Manuela had opened her heart in time, we knew we must not pursue the matter any further. Juan Valdez is a good boy. They will be happy. We drank too much that night, *mi amigo* and I. When he left here I did not realise I would never see him again.'

'That—that was the night he died. How awful,' Ysanne whispered, rising to perch herself on the arm of his chair and take his hand in hers.

'A few days after the funeral, this tired old heart of mine began to give me trouble. Felipe assumed control, as he should have done years ago. It was not to my liking, as you can imagine, but I had no choice. I hoped, prayed, he would at last become a man with so many responsibilities on his shoulders.'

Responsibilities which would have been hers had she been at home, Ysanne realised.

'He is a fool,' Diego said sourly. 'He does not like to ride horses, only to race them with his foppish friends and wager on the outcome. He likes his stomach to be full so long as he does not have to provide the food. He has a taste for good wines, but only if someone else supervises the production from grape to table. Without Hermano's help and advice the vines would have died. How I have missed you, my daughter. There was so much you did out of love for this place. I did not realise how much until I needed your strength and you were not here.'

'It shall be as it was,' Ysanne promised.

'Nothing will ever be as it was,' came the chilling reply. 'Someone, I feel sure, is out to destroy us. We have had cattle stolen, even poisoned. This episode you witnessed was only one of several, as Ruy said, where homes have been ransacked and burned. *Peónes* killed as they worked in the fields. Not only men, but women and children too. No one is safe from these fiends.'

'Our cattle? Our people only?' Ysanne ventured to ask.

'No. Ruy has lost both too and our neighbour Sancho Morales came here last week to report the loss of over twenty head of prime beef. You see why I find it difficult to attach blame?'

'Indians perhaps?'

'Have you ever heard of an Indian beating a man

to death with a whip? No, these are white men, but who they are, what they hope to gain . . .'

'Possession of the valley. You must be right,' Ysanne returned, her eyes clouding. 'Papa, do you honestly believe Ruy could be behind it all? Could he cold-bloodedly have had some of his own people killed and cattle stolen in order to make it appear he is a victim too?'

'What a question to ask!'

'You inferred the troubles did not start until after the death of Pedro Valdez, when Felipe stepped into your shoes.'

'Since the day I became ill Felipe has become master of the Hacienda de las Flores. I am rarely consulted over anything these days. It was necessary, I suppose. At least I have been able to rest and regain my strength. Now you are back we will work together again and he can go back to his idle ways. You are right, however, it all seemed to start happening after Pedro's death. Felipe asked me to approach Ruy about Manuela. You can imagine how reticent I was to do that, knowing how deeply she and Juan were in love, but he—he is my son and I agreed. Ruy rejected my offer as I expected. He was, after all, only following his father's wishes. I thought that to be an end to the matter, but Felipe refused to accept the decision. He and Juan have always disliked each other since they were children. Now he has turned his resentment, the bitterness at his disappointment, against them both. Things became—shall we say, difficult. Juan went so far as to imply that Felipe might have been responsible for his father's death. Felipe, in return, said the story was concocted out of malice, that Manuela had pledged herself to him and was being forced to marry against her will. Believe me, I am at a loss what to believe any more. It was during this time of squabbling that the first raids took place to make life more complicated.'

'Why should Felipe lie? Or why should Ruy and Juan fabricate such a story? It is beyond my comprehension too. Have they all gone mad?'

'I have asked Ruy here to settle things once and for all,' Diego murmured, squeezing her hand reassuringly. 'It was his father's wish as well as mine that the two of you should marry. I gather Ruy never knew of the plans he had made, had he lived.'

'Do you wish to be rid of me already?' It was what she wanted too, although some of the magic had gone from the great homecoming, the many plans she herself had made. Deep inside, she was suddenly afraid and she did not know why!

Diego's gaze lifted from her anxious features to the portrait of the woman on the opposite wall. Flame-red curls, skin like alabaster. The same well-defined bone structure. Pride blazed from the lovely face. She wore a deep emerald ball gown, diamonds in her ears and around her throat. Ysanne had had that dress copied with great care.

'Am I so much like her?' she asked, following his eyes. Her mother had been so beautiful! 'Always you are sad when you look at her.'

'This has not been a happy house since she died. I could only give so much. I have deprived you of many things. Perhaps I should have married again.'

'Never. Be honest, Papa, something was wrong between you even when I was a child. You favoured me. She loved Felipe. I never did understand why you and he were not closer. Has it not been resolved now? Hermano could not have run this place alone.'

'You—you are all I want. Ysanne, stay! Be my strength for a while yet. I have things to do before I allow anyone to take you from me.' Diego's fingers closed over hers so forcefully she winced in pain. 'Without you I am lost. I no longer know who to trust.'

'Trust me. Together we will find the answers,' she assured him and kissed him affectionately. 'Somehow, some way we will bring peace back to the Valle de Lágrimas.'

'I am delighted to hear you say that,' Ruy Valdez declared from the doorway behind her.

Tossing his sombrero into a chair, he advanced towards Diego. Hesitantly, she thought, but as her father smiled, he reached out and grasped the offered hand.

'You are better, I hope?'

'All the better for having Ysanne home again.'

'My friend, resourceful as she is, Ysanne cannot solve this problem all by herself,' Ruy declared gravely and instantly she bristled.

'The valley is mine,' she declared.

'Land, Ysanne. That's all it is.' He wheeled on her, his face bleak. 'Are you going to go out there and protect it personally?'

'If I have to.' There was no hesitation in her answer and she saw her father's smile grow. How dared he think otherwise?

'Then you are dead! Someone wants it badly enough to kill anyone in their way. Who, I don't know. *Dios*, I wish I did. This madman is destroying everything that has been good and stable these past thirty years. These killings cannot go on.

We must organise ourselves. If you will not join with me, then . . .'

'You will stop them yourself? What makes you think you will succeed where father and I might fail?' she challenged, and watched the anger intensify in his expression as he stared at her.

Watching them, Diego despaired of a match between them. Look at them! Like two contestants about to do battle. Yet the outcome, resolved peacefully—such prospects! What a combination of fire and strength!

'What do you intend to do, Ysanne? Strap on a gun and go looking for our troublemakers?' he taunted.

'I'm surprised you expected anything else of me,' she flung back. 'On my land there will be no further abuses of power, so you can tell the people you took away earlier that they can return at any time and they will not be molested again. Who was there during my absence to create such havoc? Who desires power so much?'

'Ysanne, sweet little sister, why were you not born a boy? Think of the pleasure that would have given our father. Such enthusiasm! Such stamina to protect what is yours. *Buenos días*, Ruy. A short visit, I trust.'

Felipe de Rivas advanced from the doorway to take Ysanne in his arms and soundly kiss her. He was stronger, more confident than the brother she had left behind, she thought, as he released her and stepped back. His grasp had proved that. Yet the same eyes still surveyed her. Dark brown, searching as always, giving her once again the impression he could see right through her. Many times during a conversation with him, she had been sure that not only did he not know with whom he was conversing, but that he was far away, totally absorbed in a world of his own.

She had always thought how much more intelligent he was than she herself, interested in things far above her head. He loved horses, never to ride or breed, which greatly annoyed their father, but to race. His stables contained only the best Arabian stallions that could be brought into the country. He adored painting, although she had never been able to understand the colourful drawings which adorned the rooms in which he lived. Somehow they always seemed unreal to her. She could not identify with them in any way and Felipe often lost patience with her when she asked for an explanation as to their meaning.

He talked of times past, when ancient civilisations ruled California, long before any white face appeared to preach God-fearing Christianity, yet he treated the *indios* on the *hacienda*, descendants most of them of the great people he admired, as beings beneath his contempt. Always he made Ysanne feel his inferior, although in her heart she knew she was not. She had proved that by stepping into the shoes he had willingly relinquished. They were equals, but she would never have dared suggest this to him. Felipe's tempers were well known, and carefully avoided by everyone.

As a child she remembered how she had always been careful to try and please him, usually without success. As they grew older, his moodiness and unpredictability increased. She could do nothing but accept it, weather the storms and later remember that the bear who had baited and abused her with a tongue of devils, struck her and once left her to ride home in atrocious weather, was still her brother. Capable of gentleness when the mood took him, of compassion, but never she suspected of love. There were times when she thought him incapable of all three. A stranger! A frightening stranger!

'Felipe. As charming—and provocative as ever.' She returned his kiss, but it was only half-hearted and she was aware of Ruy watching her with narrowed gaze.

Crossing to his side, she took his empty glass, together with her father's and refilled them both. Then she filled two more for Felipe and herself. Then, the smile fading from her face, she stood in the midst of them and demanded a toast.

'I am home now, *mi amigos*. Let us drink to the continued friendship of us all. No more enmity. We must work together, not against each other, to discover who covets my land enough to kill and destroy for it, must we not?'

It was a challenge, delivered with the full force of her personality behind it. Taken at once by Ruy who raised his glass towards her, recognising the light of battle in her eyes which he had seen many times before. Today he had not come to wage war or take up the gauntlet he knew had been deliberately flung in his direction. He had come to talk. He prayed a fight would not be forced on him, because fight he would, whatever the consequences to those standing around him.

Diego hesitated before he too slowly raised his glass in the direction of his daughter—and deliberately drained it.

Felipe! Ysanne watched and waited as he stared at her, then a familiar smile crossed his features. He emptied his glass, grabbed up the jug and refilled the four glasses.

'Welcome home, my sister. You will never know how glad I am to see you again.'

'*Por favor*, Ruy will you stay and dine with us,' Diego asked. 'We have much to talk about.'

The first of many such dinners, Ysanne hoped, however noncommittal he sounded now.

'Then you must all excuse me. I have so many presents to unpack and I need to freshen up.'

'Go, child,' her father said quietly. 'I shall speak to Rosa and ensure she sets a fine table for us today.'

The door had hardly closed behind her when the smile vanished from Diego's face. He raised himself, with some difficulty, from his chair and stared at Ruy Valdez.

'Have you come to argue with me yet again?' he demanded.

'If you two are going to have another of your stormy encounters, I am going to get myself a decent drink and retire upstairs,' Felipe interrupted rudely and left them without another word.

'Well?' Diego demanded again of the silent figure facing him. 'Don't stand there, come and look at these papers I have had drawn up. These will settle the issue at stake once and for all.'

'Does she know?'

'Not yet. She need never know if you keep your end of the bargain. There will be peace in the Valle de Lágrimas. That is the only thing she cares about.' Almost the only thing, Diego thought as Ruy advanced towards him.

* * *

The bath into which she relaxed was bliss. Her aches and bruises, the dust of the journey, floated away in the tub of hot water. She would go downstairs and face all three of them, determined in her resolve to make her precious valley safe. Tomorrow she would ride through it so that those remaining there could see she was home and they had nothing to fear. If they were in trouble, or threatened from outside, they could once again come to her.

Serafina had laid out a dark coloured skirt and a white silk blouse. On her mistress' instructions she tied back the fiery tresses with a matching ribbon. So far she had been asked no questions. She had been steeling herself deliberately to lie when the moment came, so she was relieved when Ysanne said,

'My father has explained what is happening, as far as he knows. However I am disappointed you made it necessary for him to send for me. You could have contacted me yourself long before this.'

'Don Diego would not hear of writing to you at first,' Serafina answered. *And there were those in this house who would have prevented the letter from leaving as you will soon find out, my poor baby. It is not going to be as easy as you believe to put things right.* But this she did not put into words. The time was not right.

'You have no idea who is behind the trouble, I suppose? Have you heard no gossip among the *peónes*? You have the ear of so many of the wives.'

'None, *mi niña*. Strangers from the North perhaps. For several months now there has been talk that Mexico intends to hand California over to the *Americanos*. You know what that will mean. Men will come here seeking the best land.'

'*Sí*. I remember Papa telling me there was trouble when Mexico took over this country from our native Spain. Land-grabbers came in their hundreds thinking to dispossess those already established here. It was a bad time. It is strange he did not think of that.'

One little lie. God would surely forgive her that, Serafina thought as she quickly gathered up the damp towels from the floor, aware of the girl relaxing slightly as she pondered the thought.

'Bring down those packages on the bed for me, Serafina. I want to see the look on Papa's face when he finds what I have brought him—a pair of exquisitely cut Venetian glass decanters. I bought Felipe a new riding whip with a silver top and the bolt of new cloth at the bottom of the trunk is for you.'

'And for Don Ruy? Surely you did not forget him?'

'No, I did not.' Ysanne smiled as she thought of the one present which had taken her over a month to decide upon. A skilfully carved figure of a stallion in onyx. 'What was that?' She spun around towards the door, a frown puckering her brows. 'Did you hear a cry?'

Serafina shook her head. For a moment there was no sound in the room, even the fan-tail doves outside the window became silent. Then, from somewhere below came the distinct sound of breaking glass, the overturning of heavy furniture.

Ysanne caught her breath in alarm. 'Leave those things for the moment. Come with me, quickly.'

Half-way down the stairs she heard angry voices coming from the direction of the study where she had left Ruy together with her father and brother. Through the partly open door she could see a table had been overturned and a carved chair lay broken in the hallway where curious servants had begun to gather.

She was within three steps of the door itself when she heard Felipe cry out.

'*Dios!* What have you done?'

She came to a sudden halt, the colour draining from her face as Ruy appeared in her path. His jacket was ripped in several places. One cheek was heavily bruised and she saw that the hand he raised to his mouth to wipe away a trickle of blood was grazed and bleeding. Her horrified eyes slowly moved past him to the inert figure of her father lying on the floor which was covered in broken glass, with Felipe on his knees beside him, holding fast to his hand and apparently trying without success to revive him.

'What—what have you done?' she cried echoing her brother's words, without realising what she was saying. She heard Serafina gasp behind, as Felipe looked up at them. His face too was bruised and bleeding.

'He struck him! He struck our father! Damn your eyes, Ruy Valdez, may you rot in hell for this day's work,' he swore.

Ruy's eyes blazed at his words. As Ysanne tried to push past him, he caught her by the wrist and held her fast.

'Take my advice, Ysanne, and go back to the safety of Monterey. You should never have left it. You do not belong here any longer. Stay and you will be used as a pawn in a very unpleasant game of chess.'

'I do not know what you mean. Who would use me? My father? Never!' She spat the words at him. 'Let me go! Have you taken leave of your senses?'

He cut across her words with an expletive which made her wince. She recoiled from the fury in his face. He was like a man possessed! Never had she seen him this way before.

'Felipe rules this house now, not Diego. If you stay he will destroy you,' he snapped. 'You asked who desired power enough to kill for it. I tell you now, your own brother!'

She gasped as if he had struck her.

'The Valle de Lágrimas! That's what you were fighting over, wasn't it?' Disbelief registered on her lovely face. Her own words, said only a short while ago to her father, came back to haunt her. 'There are only two people who could benefit from owning the valley. Felipe—or . . .' And her father's answer. Had he known something he had not told her? 'Ruy. That is why I place no blame. My own son or the man who is to become my son-in-law.' It could not be possible, yet if she was to believe her own eyes . . .

'You attacked an old man. A sick old man!' It was impossible to believe him capable of such an outrage, such brutality. But the truth lay before her and he was trying to blame Felipe. 'Let me go to them. I am not old, Ruy, nor ill. You will not find me so easy to deal with.'

'You little fool, you don't know what you are saying. You don't think . . . *Dios!* You do!' His mouth tightened into a bleak line and he flung her away from him so violently she almost fell. 'In the space of a few hours that is the second time you have thrown an accusation in my face. So much for the trust we once shared.'

'What lengths will you go to to become the most powerful man in Los Pinos County, Ruy?' She flung the words at him without thinking as her eyes returned to the motionless form of her father and bright tears spilled down over her cheeks.

'Whatever lengths are necessary to do what has to be done,' came the reply which chilled her to the bone.

'Get out! Get out!' She screamed the words at him. 'If you dare to show your face in this house again I will have Hermano set the dogs on you.'

Don't go, her heart begged. *Tell me I am wrong. Offer some explanation.*

For a long moment Ruy Valdez stared down into her accusing eyes, the wet cheeks and quivering lips, then without a word he strode past her and she heard him cursing under his breath. The watching servants took one look into his face and moved back, allowing him to pass unmolested. Without a word—without a backward glance, out through the door. Out of the house. Out of her life.

CHAPTER THREE

THE ROOM where Diego de Rivas lay darkened with shadows as dusk began to fall. Servants came and went with downcast eyes, no words passing between them and the silent girl seated beside the bed as they brought endless cups of coffee which were always left to grow cold, or food which remained untouched on the plate. After five hours Serafina herself took up some fresh coffee and a plate of honeyed pancakes which Rosa had especially prepared, in the hope of enticing her mistress to eat. She had touched nothing since supper the night before.

Ysanne stared at the tray with dull eyes and shook her head. Undaunted, Serafina thrust the cup under her nose, totally ignoring the daggered look she received.

'Drink it, *mi niña*. Do you want to help him, or frighten him to death by fainting from hunger under his very nose? *Bueno!* Now start on the pancakes while I pour another cup.'

It was an effort, but somehow Ysanne managed to force down every mouthful of the food, without her usual appreciation of the pancakes which were her personal favourite. The coffee revived her. Serafina's interruption into her solitude had roused her to instant anger, but now, more alert, she knew it had been necessary.

'Where is my brother?'

'I persuaded him to eat something too. Shall I fetch him?'

'There is nothing he can do. Nothing I can do. Oh, Serafina, I feel so helpless. Look at him lying there so still. He has not moved once since we carried him up here. Felipe fears the unprovoked attack on him may have brought on another seizure. I have been sitting here thinking this is all a dream, that I will awake in a few moments to find us all in the study . . . I could not believe my eyes! Did you see Ruy? That murderous look in his eyes?'

'*Sí*, I saw him. Looking like *el diablo* himself as he stood before you. Such a temper that one has.'

'I know it. But to strike down an old man, a friend he knew was in ill health! I must know what passed between them to bring this about.'

'I can tell you, although you will not like the truth.' Her brother had entered the room so quietly, neither of the women became aware of his presence until he stepped past Serafina and stared down at his unconscious father. 'Has he not moved? Spoken?'

'Nothing. Hold me, Felipe, I am so afraid,' Ysanne begged and he came to her side and put his arms around her. 'Tell me. I want to know every word that passed between you downstairs. Don't spare me. I have to know what happened.'

'Come away from the bed then, lest we disturb him. Come,' he urged as she hesitated, 'the doctor should be here soon. He was obviously out on another call when Fernando arrived, or he would have been here by now. Until he arrives, we can do nothing. Serafina, stay close to Don Diego.'

'*Sí, señor.*' The woman lowered herself into a

chair. Wild horses could not have dragged her away!

Felipe led Ysanne out into the corridor and out through the open french windows onto the balcony where he had previously been sitting.

'There is much you have to know and it is not pleasant,' he said as she seated herself tentatively on the edge of one of the cane chairs. 'But as you insist on knowing everything . . .'

'Then for heaven's sake, tell me,' she interrupted. Her nerves, already frayed from the earlier incident were strung out still further by the collapse of her father. She looked at the smile on Felipe's boyish features and her lips tightened. 'You look like a cat who has just stolen the cream. You are going to enjoy this, I know it.'

'As blunt as always, but wrong this time. Very wrong. For months now I have been forced to put up a front, a defensive shield. I have almost forgotten what it is like to be myself. I am civil to those who are rude to me, I smile at those I know speak ill of me behind my back and while I am doing these things, I watch and listen and learn much they would rather I did not know.'

'They? Who? You are talking in riddles,' Ysanne interrupted again, raising a hand to her throbbing temples. 'Do you know who is causing the trouble?'

'At this moment I only suspect. I have no proof.' Leaning back in his chair, Felipe produced a long cheroot and proceeded to light it, prolonging her suspense still further. His eyes considered her for a long moment through a cloud of grey smoke.

He was still exceedingly pale, but more in control of himself than she was, Ysanne realised. He had grown up a great deal during the time she had been away. There would be people accustomed to dealing with her father over matters concerning the ranch who would not take kindly to being forced to negotiate with Felipe, for whom many had neither liking nor respect, considering him to be a wastrel and a fool, incapable of responsibility or trust. Had it taken their father's illness to make him realise he was capable of both?

'Before I point the finger in any direction, you must know how it all began. I suspect today was the culmination of many months of frustration and thwarted planning for someone, which is why it ended so violently. However, let us go back many months . . . In a way I fear I may have been to blame for some of this because of my love for Manuela. My feelings have been used as an excuse by those who wish to see me destroyed.'

'Isn't she to marry Juan Valdez?'

'She loves me! Has always loved me, but they did not think me good enough!' The smile faded and his voice grew harsh. 'Don Pedro Valdez and the illustrious Ruy, who was his father's right hand and instrumental I know in ensuring we did not marry. What malice that serpent must have whispered into the old man's ears in order to have his own way. Nothing happens today that Ruy does not know about; is not behind.'

'Are you accusing him?' Ysanne began incredulously. She had been praying that this moment would never come, that it had all been some ghastly mistake.

'*Dios!* What proof do you need? You saw him, heard what he said,' Felipe flung at her, eyes burning with deep anger. 'His own words condemned him. No, for you there must be more, of course.

Forgive me, my sister, it pains me to continue, but I must if you are to learn the truth about the man you love. Realise the power and ambition he craves and believe the lengths he will go to to have what he wants.'

Any lengths that are necessary to do what has to be done. Ysanne inwardly shivered as she remembered Ruy's words, and recalled the look in those eyes. He was not the same! Nor was her brother. No more was she—now! The pain in her heart was like the slow twisting of a sharp dagger. Felipe was about to condemn the man she loved by giving her the proof she demanded and his words would inflict more unhealable wounds. Nothing but Ruy's denial could ease her suffering, but he had chosen to turn his back on her and walk away. The act of a guilty man!

'Go on,' she said dully.

'First I must acquaint you with the fact that I am suspected of being the murderer of Don Pedro.'

She could only stare at him in disbelief. At last she found herself stammering,

'Murderer! What—what nonsense. You! Besides Father said it was an accident.'

'We argued that night, the three of us, over Manuela. Father had promised to speak out on my behalf, but he didn't. I had to do it myself. Manuela and I were already making plans for our future . . . *Dios mío*, when her hand was refused me I could not believe it, then Don Pedro revealed that he and Ruy had discussed the match the night before. Ruy had persuaded him that Juan loved her and was more suitable.'

'Father said you lost your temper.'

'Do you blame me? I saw all the plans Manuela

and I had made slipping away in front of my eyes.'
As hers were doing now, Ysanne thought, wincing as his words twisted the knife inside her once again. 'I hardly remember what I said in my anger. I do remember begging them, Ysanne, on my bended knees to let me marry the woman I adore and still they refused me. I do not blame Father. He really tried, but you know how Don Pedro always listened to Ruy. It was a week after the old man's funeral, I remember. Dr Sanchez had confined Father to bed and I had taken over the running of the *rancho*. For the first time we were close, my sister. After so long apart. I felt such pride . . .'

'Oh, Felipe, it does my heart good to hear you say such a thing,' Ysanne said, blinking back a rush of tears to her eyes. 'It was what Papa always wanted.'

'Somehow I was never able to tell him how dearly I wished for it too. Then it was happening.' Felipe flicked the ash from his cheroot on to the floor. The handsome features grew taut with agitation as he continued. 'About that time I heard the rumour that Don Pedro had not fallen from his horse, but had been waylaid and struck down. After what happened, the argument, I mean, I was naturally the prime suspect. I had a watertight alibi however. Nothing Juan Valdez said could alter that.'

'Juan actually accused you of murdering his father? Felipe, this is all so incredible. He is the most shy boy I have ever known. Incapable, I am sure, of malice, or, as you indicate, vindictiveness. He has Manuela. Why should he so falsely accuse you?'

'Dear Ysanne, still so naïve. Has your time in a big city not taught you anything? Manuela loved the old man like a father. Turning her against me was a sure way of making her accept the match that he and Ruy have arranged for her.'

'Ruy! Always Ruy! You have no proof he had a hand in these arrangements any more than that he is behind the trouble now.'

'Juan has Manuela. When—had—you married Ruy, he would have controlled the valley through you. Perhaps he has plans for making Pinos Altos and this place into one huge *estancia*. It would make it the largest estate in this part of the country. What power then, eh?'

'You forget, even when I am married the valley still remains in my possession. Under my control, until I sign it over to my daughter,' Ysanne said tremulously. Such questions crowding into her mind. Answers to none of them so far.

'Or to your son! Grow up, Ysanne. You love the man. Are you telling me that, trusting him completely, you could not be persuaded to sign it over to him—or the next male heir. That man could make you do anything. For love of him you left here, did you not? Went into self-imposed exile in order to return an attractive, enticing woman. One he would notice! I think I preferred you as you were. Silks and frills are all very becoming, but they are not the real Ysanne. Beneath all those fripperies I hope there is still the strength and determination you possessed before, because you are going to need it. It showed before and although I probably never told you, I admired it. Now I have a little more of my own. I realise that together we can beat everyone who opposes us. The Hacienda de las Flores will be the greatest *rancho* around here, with you and I running it.'

'Who—who told you why I went away?' Ysanne asked through trembling lips. The nightmare was growing worse. He painted Ruy as a power-hungry devil, dealing out death and destruction to all those who opposed him. Her brother was presumed to be a murderer. Her father lay unconscious in his bed . . .

'Father, of course. We have no secrets from each other now. Besides, when he became ill, I wanted to bring you home immediately. He had to tell me everything in order to stop me writing to you. Eventually I managed to persuade him to write himself and tell you to come back. What a stupid idea! Make yourself attractive for Ruy Valdez. He is not worthy to kiss the dust you walk over. There are a dozen men more eligible.'

'I love him. I want only him,' Ysanne said, getting to her feet. 'Don't treat me like a child, Felipe.'

'My dear, I would not insult your intelligence by doing so. However it seems neither of us is to have what we want in life, so we will have to make the best of each other, won't we?'

'I do not like this talk of us running the place when Father is lying ill in bed.'

'I mean, of course, we shall have to take care of things until he is better,' Felipe returned. 'If he recovers . . .'

'What—what do you mean? You said he fell . . .'

'From a blow Ruy delivered with such force he was knocked backwards into the table. I am not sure if he hit his head against the edge of the desk as he went down. I grappled with Ruy, but he has three times my strength. He simply threw me aside.

And then you came downstairs. It is possible your appearance saved me from a beating. Father is not strong, Ysanne. You must prepare yourself for the worst. Another seizure could kill him.'

'Why did Ruy strike him?' she demanded.

'I only came in on the tail end of the conversation. I know nothing of what passed between them while I was in the *sala*. I came back in time to hear Ruy tell Father I had been seen—Juan had seen me, to be correct—with the men who burned that village today. I denied it, of course. Do you believe, if I were responsible, I would have allowed my face to be seen? This shows you the extent of his hatred. His determination to destroy me so that Manuela will turn to him. I tell you, little sister, this devilish plot goes deep and it is cleverly planned, taking everything into account, even my love for Manuela and Father's illness. We are all being manipulated by that man.'

'I must go back to Papa,' Ysanne said, turning away.

She was trembling visibly, fighting to keep back the tears. He made Ruy sound such a monster, bent on destroying them all in the quest for power. He had always had a masterful way about him, so sure of himself and everything he did, but to crave power enough to kill for it? Ruin the lives of so many people? No! He had never shown any inclination towards that. Could he have changed so drastically in six months? She had already noticed he had altered in his attitude towards her. Distant, almost suspicious. Had she ever really known him at all?

'So you love him still.' Felipe sighed as he took her by the shoulders and stared into her distraught features. 'It is a cross you must bear by yourself. I will fight him alone if I have to. What a fool idea it was giving the valley to a woman anyway! Illogical minds, ruled by emotions instead of common sense . . .'

'On the way home, Ruy too, commented on my inability to protect what is mine. He asked if I would take a gun to defend it,' Ysanne's temper was immediately roused by the unfair comment. 'If necessary, I will.'

'Even against him?' Her brother asked, a smile creasing the thin white scar at the corner of his mouth. She did not like that smile.

It was the way he had looked that day he deliberately turned loose all the horses from the stables after being confined to his room for refusing to continue with his riding lessons. Diego's prize stallions had galloped away to freedom. It had taken a dozen men to round them up again. One had broken a leg and had to be shot. Felipe had never been punished. He had gone before their father, at thirteen years of age, and sworn that a young Mexican lad had not secured the gate properly. And he had been believed. The boy had been flogged and Felipe had watched. He had smiled then too! Her indignant stand in defence of the poor unfortunate had been laughed at. If she went to their father and betrayed him, he would only deny it again, he told her. Ysanne had only been six years old at the time, but she had never forgotten that smile.

She had seen it many times since. It always made her suspect that her brother in some way enjoyed the discomfort of others, especially if he had a hand in it.

'If it becomes necessary,' she forced the words through stiff lips.

'Forgive me, but I don't believe you. I do not mean that unkindly. You are shocked and upset. When this is past you will think only of what is in your heart. This momentary pain will be forgotten.' His attention was caught by something outside and he quickly released her. 'Horsemen have just arrived. Dr Sánchez at last! Go back to Father, I will meet him and explain.'

As Ysanne entered her father's bedroom, a low, distinct moan came from the direction of the bed and she called urgently to her brother as she saw his eyelids begin to flutter open.

'Felipe, quickly. I think Papa is regaining consciousness.' He followed her into the room immediately and Serafina moved away as they both bent over the injured man. 'Papa, you are all right! Don't move, the doctor will be here in a moment.' Tears streamed down over Ysanne's cheeks and fell on the cheek upon which she bestowed a loving kiss.

'Such a—welcome—home for my daughter,' Diego's words were barely audible.

'Hush. Save your strength,' she insisted, gripping his hands tightly. How cold they were! How strange his eyes looked. Wary. No, afraid, or was it both? Of course he was afraid. He had been struck down in his own house by someone he had always considered a friend. Treachery had so many faces! How many more did Ruy possess that she knew nothing of?

'It—it was an accident.'

The words were very faint, but distinct, and her startled eyes flew to her brother's face. Felipe bent forward, a hand on her shoulder, motioning her to remain silent.

'Father, how can you say that? The man deliberately hit you and in a most violent manner because you defended me. I thank you for that, although to save this happening, I would rather you had not. I have told Ysanne everything. We have no need to pretend further. He is trying to protect you still, my sister. Tell him it is not necessary.'

'Felipe is right. You must keep nothing from me in the future and you must no longer worry about me,' she whispered.

Diego's head rolled from side to side on the pillow. Words fell from his lips, but were too incoherent for either of them to understand. His agitation greatly alarmed Ysanne, who could do nothing to calm him.

'Let me.' Felipe moved her to one side and taking his father by the shoulders, held him fast, at the same time putting his ear close to his mouth. Ysanne saw his face grow pale and tense. When he stood back from the bed, he did not look at her, but at his father who was silent and still once more.

'What—what did he say?' she pleaded.

'More pain for you,' Felipe's tone held an odd note. 'No, those were not his words, that is what they will bring. Over and over again he repeated—"Ruy has won".'

Ysanne recoiled as if he had struck her and Serafina hurried forward to put a comforting arm around her shoulders. Condemned, from her father's own lips! It was no good trying to convince herself further. He was guilty!

'Bring Dr Sánchez, quickly,' Felipe said urgently, propelling her to the door. 'You! Serafina.

Make sure there is a hot meal ready when he comes downstairs. He has come a long way. He may even stay overnight. Be sure there is a room prepared also.'

Ysanne ran from the room with Serafina close on her heels. Felipe did not wait to see them reach the bottom of the stairs. Closing the door, he turned back towards the bed.

'Now, Father,' he said quietly. 'It is time you had some rest.'

'I'm sorry.' The doctor stared into the face of the woman before him, so controlled in her grief now after the tears which had greeted him upon his arrival. 'There was nothing I could do. This last attack was too severe. Don Felipe said he used the last of his strength trying to speak.'

'The blow to his head was not—was not the cause of his death, then?'

'The shock of it most certainly brought about the seizure and, with all due respect, Doña Ysanne, your return probably caused him great excitement. I warned him at all times to remain quiet and calm. The combination of the two . . . *Quién sabe?*'

'Are you saying I am as responsible as the man who struck him down?' Ysanne cried aghast.

'No, my child, I am saying your father's heart had undergone too much stress and tension this—these past few years. At the most, with all the love and care you could have given him, his time would have been very short.'

'How—how long?'

'A few months more.'

He had known he was dying when he wrote to her! Mutely Ysanne nodded, accepting what he said. Her eyes were dry of tears. Her features showed none of the terrible grief she was experiencing. She wanted to cry, but could not. Dead! Her beloved father was dead! She had wasted six months of her life away from his side, deprived him of her company, her love—all for a dream that would never be realised. Ruy Valdez would never know she loved him now. Never be told why she went away. There would be no marriage. The dream was shattered! Her love destroyed—betrayed!

'Serafina will take you downstairs. Please stay and have something to eat before you go.'

Dr Sánchez took the slender fingers offered and politely shook them, marvelling at the inward strength she possessed at such a time. Although not a close friend, he had known Diego de Rivas for several years and was fully aware of the close relationship shared by father and daughter.

'If there is anything I can do . . .' he began.

'You are very kind. There is nothing,' Ysanne said dully. 'My brother and I will do whatever is necessary.'

Whatever is necessary! Those words would haunt her until the day she died. Like a sleepwalker she turned back into the room where her father lay. The doctor had drawn the sheet over Diego's face, but Felipe had pulled it back again. She caught her brother's hand in a tight grip.

'Help me,' she whispered brokenly. 'I am so confused, afraid. I cannot think for myself any more.'

'We must help each other. Fight together. There must be no dissension between us ever again,' Felipe said in a low, fierce tone and she nodded, realising what he too had lost. He had been deprived of their father just as they were beginning to grow close for the first time since he was a child.

'I will keep what is mine, or die protecting it. I swear it,' she said and his eyes narrowed as he turned to look at her. 'Yes, against Ruy, Juan, anyone who dares to think they can take what belongs to me—to us.'

'Then—you are not going to marry him?'

'Marry him!' Ysanne's green eyes widened in horror and her whole being rebelled at the thought of giving herself to the man who had struck down her father. His white, marble features swam before her tortured vision. 'Marry the man who murdered my father? Never!'

Serafina heard the agonising cry as she was returning from the kitchen. When she reached the bedroom, Ysanne lay on a day-bed beneath the window and her brother was beside her, staring out at the distant sunset. He was smiling, the woman saw. At what was beyond her. His father lay dead in his bed and his sister had collapsed from the strain of the day. One short day and so much had taken place. It was as if an evil cloud had settled over the *hacienda*, affecting all those who dwelled within its walls. She had heard such things today! Things she dare not relate to anyone, except perhaps the local priest who might absolve her from the guilt her silence would evoke.

'My sister has need of you, woman. Stay with her.' Felipe suddenly straightened, aware he was under observation, and the smile died from his face as he strode past her.

What else did he think she was in the house for? Serafina muttered under her breath as she took one of Ysanne's cold hands in hers and began to try and revive her. Acting the master already. His sister would have something to say about that. Of all of them, she was the only one who had not changed one iota in the past six months.

In the days which led up to the funeral of Diego de Rivas, Serafina began to wonder if she had not been a little hasty in her assumptions. The day after her father's death, Ysanne did not venture outside her rooms, refusing to see anyone who called, even Father Simón, the priest from the Mission at San José or friends calling to pay their last respects— even her brother. Only Serafina came and went unchallenged, her heart aching at the sound of her mistress' continual crying. She waited patiently, expectantly, for her to turn to the one person who had always been at her side when needed, but this time it did not happen. Ysanne cried herself to sleep alone and Serafina, seated in a chair by the window, unnoticed, unwanted, was deeply disturbed.

The next day she was up and dressed before Serafina arrived with her breakfast tray. The sombre black gown she wore accentuated her pallor, defined more distinctly the grey shadows beneath dull, lustreless eyes. She was withdrawn, uncommunicative almost to the point of rudeness—as never before. She spent several hours closeted with her brother in the library. When a band of armed men rode away from the *hacienda*, she watched them in silence, her face impassive—cold! Offering no explanation until Serafina, through frustration, asked the meaning of their departure.

They had gone to defend the Valle de Lágrimas, she was told. Each day it would be patrolled by armed guards who had orders to kill anyone who tried to molest the *peónes* living and working there. Men from the Hacienda de las Flores would protect her inheritance, she added, by any means necessary.

She had made her decision and there was no turning back, Ysanne thought as she lay in bed the night before the funeral. She was to be told of whatever decisions Felipe took, but apart from that, she had given him free rein to do whatever he thought necessary to apprehend the men, or man, determined to ruin the tranquillity of their peaceful existence.

People had come and gone from the house, but she had been unaware of them. Faces and names had registered, but her answers had become almost mechanical. She gave orders for the servants to prepare spare rooms for mourners who might wish to stay overnight, went through the lists of food and wines which would be consumed after the funeral, spent hours praying beside her father's body—all in a dream world. Only when she awoke on the day he was to be buried—taken from her forever—did she begin to come back to life again.

The pain of her loss was unbearable, yet somehow she forced herself over it as she began to dress. The pain which tore at her heart made her want to break down and weep, yet in a solitary moment she found she was still unable to give way to the relief of tears.

The house was so quiet. The windows of her bedroom were thrown open wide to receive a fresh morning breeze, but no sound invaded the room. The forge was closed and silent. The children remained indoors. No smell of baking from the kitchen this morning for it had all been done the night before. The house was full of people who had been arriving for hours. So far Felipe had received them alone. Ysanne knew she had to go downstairs, yet still she lingered on the balcony, her gaze centred on the deserted scene below. Never before had she seen it so desolate!

The people had been deprived of a benevolent patron. She had lost a father. The vineyards and fields beyond the walls of the house were absent of workers. They would all be at the funeral, paying their last respects to the man who had fed and clothed and housed them, some since the day they were born. She would need every one of them in the days ahead. They must all fight together in the interests of survival. Felipe was often too brusque, too aloof with them as he always had been. In a few days she would speak to them, make them realise what was at stake for them all. Fighting alone, they would accomplish nothing. Each and every one of them had to be made to understand what they could lose if the valley passed into the possession of someone else—by force of arms or otherwise.

Should she die without leaving a female heir to inherit it, the land would pass to Felipe as her next surviving relative. Had she been married, it would have become the possession of Ruy Valdez!

She had dressed that morning scarcely aware of what she was doing, refused breakfast and then gone to sit out on the balcony to compose herself for the ordeal to come. No matter how deeply she loved her home and brother, neither of them could replace what she had been deprived of. The man she loved, the house which would have been her domain, the children . . . She had lain awake trying to analyse her feelings for him. Her heart ached whenever she said his name silently to herself, remembering the times they had shared together, dwelt on what might have been. She loved him still. How was that possible?

And then she thought of that terrible day, the day of her return which should have been a happy time, but was instead one of sorrow and destruction. When they had come face to face outside the study he had been a frightening stranger and when she discovered what had happened, she thought she hated him. Love and hate, the two emotions were bound together as one and she could no longer deny the truth to herself. She loved him, but she feared him, hated the animal in him which had struck down her father and perhaps caused his death. To look on him again would cause her pain—great pain—yet she knew she must never show it lest he construed it as weakness on her part and tried to use it against her. He had so many faces she had never dreamed possible, or was it in the simplicity of first love that she had never wanted to look further? He had always been perfect to her despite the unpredictability of his moods, because she wanted him to be.

Now it was different. She had been forced to grow up overnight and her eyes were wide open, unhampered by the mists of love which made everything perfect—everything possible.

Felipe needed her. He must be uppermost in her mind. Together they would retain what belonged to them by right, against all those who opposed them, no matter who it was. She was done with childish dreams!

Her decision was irrevocable. With a sigh she rose to her feet, paused for a moment to compose herself, then made her way downstairs, forcing her mind to function so that she could converse rationally, forcing her legs to hold her when she longed to collapse in a tearful heap.

One of the first people to come forward offering quiet words of consolation and sympathy was Sancho Morales, whose *hacienda* lay to the north on the borders of the de Rivas lands. Like Pedro Valdez, he had been a frequent visitor to the house when her father was alive. A widower in his fifties who lived alone, she suspected the friendship of the other two men had greatly relieved an otherwise boring existence.

'Doña Ysanne, what can I say?' He was a gentleman from the past, she thought, looking into the distinguished features, now shadowed with concern, as he took her fingers and touched them lightly to his lips. More at home in Córdoba or Madrid than the wilderness that was California. His house was full of ancestral portraits, suits of armour, weaponry. The residence of a man absorbed in the past, if not obsessed by it. Yet she liked him and had enjoyed many an interesting conversation with him while her father and Pedro were involved in some discussion after dinner, usually on how to extend their existing properties. Once there had even been talk of merging the two. She would have only a short time in his company however, for often Felipe appeared to whisk him away, launching into more excursions into the past. They both revelled in discussing the splendours of the old country, the brilliance, the strength, the flamboyance that had once been Spain. Yet neither wished to return there to live. They had put down roots elsewhere, too strong now to relinquish.

'Will you allow me to be your friend, as I was your father's?'

'Are you not already my friend, Don Sancho? I would not wish you to be otherwise,' she answered truthfully and the grey eyes registered instant pleasure she had not expected.

More faces converged on her and he moved away. She regretted his leaving. For a moment she had felt strangely at peace in his company—protected. That was the way it should have been with Ruy, not with a man who considered her in the same light as he would his own daughter. The anger and frustration returned once more and with it, a terrible sense of foreboding. So much had happened—what more was there? Felipe took her hand and she moved with him around the room to greet the people present as was her duty, while all she longed for was the sanctuary of her room.

The small plot of land where all the de Rivas family were buried was a mile from the house on the slopes of a hill. Beneath sweet-smelling firs and pines, Ysanne's grandparents lay at rest. Diego de Rivas would lie a few feet from his wife Carla, who had died at the young age of thirty-three after a short but fatal illness.

Together again, Ysanne thought, as she bent to throw a handful of earth on to the coffin below her. Once they had been close. Perhaps in death their differences, whatever they were, could be resolved. Felipe put a hand gently on her arm and drew her back. Her fingers closed tightly over his, but there was no response. As yet he was unaccustomed to having a sister, she thought, not minding.

As a child, he always chose to sit alone, often resenting, she had suspected, the easy way in which she slipped into the place he had vacated at her father's side. It had not been her fault, but she understood his reluctance to accept her again as his equal. And then he looked at her and smiled and tucked her arm beneath his.

'You have the heart of a lion and the bearing of a queen, my sister,' he said softly. 'How proud I am to have you by my side.'

'My brother too, has strength I never suspected,' she returned, his compliment boosting her failing morale. Custom demanded she must now return to the house and mingle with the mourners—and then last of all there would be the formalities with the lawyer. She was dreading that.

'*Permitamé.*' Sancho Morales stood at their side, offering her his arm. Felipe handed her to him with a slight nod which indicated approval. She heard the sudden raising of voices in the crowd behind them as they moved towards the waiting carriages, turned in time to see Felipe reeling backwards into the arms of one of the *vaqueros*. Confronting him was Ruy Valdez, with Juan beside him, an arm protectingly around the shoulders of a pretty brunette whose cheeks were bright with embarrassed colour.

Ysanne started towards them. Her footsteps faltered—stopped. Her disbelieving eyes looked away, clouded with bright tears, then returned brimming with anger and contempt to the tall figure standing beside the horses. She would forgive his companions their presence in her hour of grief. She liked Manuela, and Juan was young and headstrong, easily led, she suspected, by the older brother he adored, who could do no wrong in his eyes. The brother she held responsible for the death of her father.

'How many times do I have to tell you to keep your hands off her,' she heard Ruy snap and as Felipe straightened, his face a white mask of indecision, she saw the former's hand fall to the gun at his waist.

Something snapped inside her head. She brushed aside Sancho's restraining hand, did not even hear the whispered words intended to calm her.

'Haven't you done enough already, Ruy?' People fell back allowing her to pass, and there were many curious glances at the strangeness of her tone. She had eyes for one man only. 'You have already killed my father. Is it your intention to take my brother from me too?'

CHAPTER FOUR

She wanted to say more, but the words refused to come. His audacity was beyond her comprehension. To show himself here, at the funeral! She was totally unaware of the speculation she had aroused, the muttered comments behind gloved hands and fluttering fans; the amazed looks directed her way. Murder! She caught the whispered word and only then realised what she had done. Before everyone she had openly accused Ruy Valdez of murder! He was staring at her as if she had taken leave of her senses. Two black brands of fire burned into her very soul, daring her to repeat her words.

'Doña Ysanne,' Sancho said in a low tone. 'I have been presented with all the facts by your brother. I have also heard Ruy's version of what happened. There are two sides to every story, my dear,' he added quickly as she wheeled on him, rising instinctively to Felipe's defence. 'You have made a very serious accusation for which you have no proof—and no just cause. Your grief has overwhelmed you. Believe me, Ruy has no case to answer in a court of law.'

'Only in the eyes of God. In my eyes,' she flung back. Sancho had not only been her father's friend, but he was the local *alcalde*, the judge. Highly respected by everyone in the town of Mezina, which was the only decently civilised habitation for over one hundred miles. She knew she had no reason to dispute his words, but at the same time her whole being rebelled at accepting them. She had seen Ruy as he left the study that day. She had looked into his eyes and been afraid, as she was now. Two sides? Never! There was only the truth.

As a result of the blow he had delivered, her father had died. It was an indisputable fact. Ruy had committed an act of violence towards a man who had always been his friend. He had deprived her father of life, and destroyed hers! At that moment she did not know if she was seeking revenge for him or herself. The two were inseparable, driving her on like a woman possessed.

'I know the way you all feel about my brother; a wild and unpredictable disposition.' Her voice rang out loud and clear and brought immediate silence. 'I have heard the rumours which have been spread while I was away. I despair that close friends, people who have known my family for years, could accuse him of such actions . . .'

'Ysanne, sweet little sister, do not distress yourself this way.' Felipe came to her, took her hand in his and held it tight. There was blood at the corner of his mouth where he had been struck and nothing could have revived more vividly for her the events of the day she came home.

She drew a handkerchief from her purse and wiped it away. His fingers curled more tightly over hers as if in gratitude. His grip was painful, but she did not try to disengage herself, aware of the tensions which surely must have hold of him at this moment. He had been openly assaulted, humiliated, on the very day he should have been receiving the sympathy of everyone present.

'Hear me, all of you.' Her voice did not falter. 'I stand beside my brother now in his hour of need and in the future. The house of de Rivas will not, as so many of you hope, be parted by innuendos and lies.'

'They are not lies, Ysanne.' Ruy stepped towards her, shrugging off Juan's restraining hands. His face was a mask, unreadable. He was without pity for her dilemma.

'What do you know of truth? You stand there a free man after causing the death of my father! To me you killed him as surely as if you had plunged a knife into his heart. There is no justice left in this country any more or you would be brought to account for what you have done.'

The words tumbled recklessly from her lips. Her father lay in the ground at her feet. Ruy Valdez stood before her, alive—and free. The conflicting pain which tore her in two was scarcely bearable. The only way she could surmount it and control herself before the sea of watching faces, was to lash at him with a tongue which did not belong to her, stare at him with eyes that contained contempt and loathing and belonged to another woman. The empty shell of a woman who days before had touched the stars with her dreams and fantasies, only to be brought back to earth by the harshness of the reality about her.

'Be careful,' her brother whispered. 'He will twist every word you say. Use it to his own advantage before everyone here. Stay calm, my sister. There is nothing we can do yet. Sancho has made it quite plain that it is my word against Ruy's.'

'And mine,' she looked at him despairingly.

'You saw nothing. It was over by the time you

came downstairs. Thank God, Sancho used his influence to speak on my behalf or I might be in some stinking gaol by now.' He glared at the man confronting them. 'He did his best to put me there. With me out of the way, Juan married to Manuela—and you in need of comfort . . . *Dios!* The deviousness of his mind is beyond me. Look at me, Ysanne.'

The eyes she raised to his were devoid of all emotion, yet in the depths of those green pools was the hell in which she dwelled and a deep frown creased his brows as he stared at her.

'You and I are brother and sister, but we have never been as close as we are at this moment. Because of this I tell you to search your own heart and do whatever it dictates. If you love him still, go to him. I will not hold it against you. If it is possible for you to find happiness with him, then you have my blessing. I have failed you in the past. If he is your salvation, then grasp what is offered with both hands and forget about me.'

'No!' Ysanne interrupted, clinging to him. He had failed her! She had always been more than a little afraid of his strange ways, never understanding them, but the blood they shared bound them together and today they were one as never before. They had both grown up. 'Do you think I would desert you now? Think only of myself?'

'Only if you believe me capable of—murder.' The words were softly spoken and did not reach the ears of anyone else. 'Of Pedro Valdez—and our own father. Don't you see how he planned it all? He turned his father's accidental death into a murder inquiry. Now he has seen a way to be rid of me altogether. Ysanne, you would be left to run the *quinta* all alone; unprotected. Ruy is strong, persuasive—and you love him.'

'You are wrong.' She blinked back a momentary weakness of tears, touched his bruised mouth with a gentle brushing of her fingers that brought instant warmth to his eyes. 'Whatever I felt is dead. Do you hear me? I bury it now with our father. I will never again be swayed by my emotions. I will do what is best for—for the *hacienda*, for us, Felipe.'

'*Dios!* Together we are invincible.'

Such a strange look blazed in his brown eyes. Invincible! Forsaking everyone, everything save that which was good for the Hacienda de las Flores. For them! It was an alarming thought. A lonely thought, but the decision had been made.

'Ysanne.' The harsh tones belonged to Ruy Valdez. 'For the love of heaven, listen to me before it is too late.'

'For you? I saw you. The look on your face . . .'

He cursed her under his breath and she watched Manuela turn away, heard the ripple of amazement which ran through the onlookers. I have seen him this way before, she thought. I have seen and endured his moments of temper, the devil that rides on his back when he comes in conflict with people who oppose him. I was not frightened then, nor am I now. I wish I was. I wish I could turn and run, leave everything to Felipe, be the weak female he expects me to be. I am not. I never will be. If he fights Felipe, he fights me!

'You will not listen.' It was framed as a statement, not a question. When she shook her head he swore again. 'You little fool! I am trying to protect you. Hear me out. It was your father's last wish that I protect you.'

'Protect me?' Her scornful tone brought a flush of deep colour into his aquiline features. 'Since when have I needed your protection, Ruy Valdez?' How dare he mention her father, who had known better than anyone how resourceful she was. She had always been strong, the one ruled by her head, not her heart—until she had fallen in love and learned the heartache unrequited love could bring. 'You always told me what a capable person I was. Such an attribute to my father's house because I thought like a man instead of a weak-minded woman. You insulted my brother even then without me realising it, or what motive lay behind your words.

'Motive,' he echoed. 'You believed his fairy tales? You believe it was me who struck your father? Six months in Monterey have dulled your wits, my little peacock. Felipe hit Diego, not me. His desire for power is endless. He will go to any ends to achieve it. You will be sacrificed along with everyone else if you get in his way. You are as dispensable as your father! As mine!'

'Felipe is my brother.' His words stunned her. They were delivered with such force she had to use every ounce of stamina to counteract the impact they had on her. Out of the corner of her eye she saw Sancho move closer, protectively, towards her and watched Ruy's eyes narrow as he too, became aware of the figures beginning to group in opposition in front of him. 'Have I not made it quite clear? His will is mine.'

They stood only a few feet apart, like two war lords about to do battle. Alone on a great plain despite the people about them. Both convinced they were in the right. It was unnerving!

'Are you prepared to die for a madman?' Ruy demanded and his words broke the last remaining threads of her composure. She looked at him, oblivious to the staring people on each side of her, oblivious to what they thought or said, oblivious to the sensation she was about to cause. Her words would bind her to Felipe, show him the depth of her love, her determination to stand by him whatever happened. Show the man before her the depth of her loathing for him.

'Shall I tell you about madness, Ruy?' She hesitated for a moment only. She had to purge herself of this sickness that possessed her. Cleanse her soul. It would not stop her loving him, but that was her own private hell which she must endure alone. 'I have loved you since I was fourteen years old. To you, I was a tousle-headed tomboy who would ride with you and Juan, and we enjoyed those rides, did we not, without either of you ever considering me to be what I was—a woman! I left my home for you. I went to Monterey to learn how to be a good wife and mother, how to please the man I had chosen to spend the rest of my life with. I return to find my land ravaged by *bandidos*, my people deprived of their livelihood, their homes. The man I respected and honoured above all others, had killed my father; accused my brother of the vilest of crimes. My heart cries out for vengeance. Do you hear that, Ruy? Vengeance against those who have deprived me of what I love most. My heart is empty. You have left me nothing. It seems to be your way. An eye for an eye, is what I want! Your life for that of my father.'

If she had taken her brother's gun and shot him, her words could not have had a more devastating effect. For a long moment he stared at her in silence, his face white, the mouth drawn into a bleak line. His eyes devoured her soul, challenged her words. She met them, held their gaze and won, for it was he who turned away without a word, vaulted astride the waiting horse and rode out of sight without looking back once. He had brought a dozen or more *vaqueros* with him. Half of them followed in his wake, the remainder stayed to escort Juan and Manuela safely away from the funeral grounds. Exactly as he had done that day at the house, she remembered. He had no defence against her words. The knowledge chilled her to the bone. Guilty as charged!

'Come, Doña Ysanne.' Sancho Morales took her hand from Felipe and led her to the closed carriage.

'Please—stay with me. I need your strength,' she faltered and he smiled and helped her inside.

'I shall always be at your side if you wish it.'

Only when Serafina had put her to bed that night and she had lain awake for several hours, did she begin to ponder the significance of his words.

'You have been seeing a great deal of Sancho Morales these past few weeks,' Felipe said to the pale-faced girl who sat opposite him at dinner, the severity of her black gown broken only by a single strand of pearls about her throat.

'I like his company,' Ysanne answered, pushing aside the plate in front of her, with most of the food still untouched. She ate very little these days. 'But if you don't approve . . .'

'My dear girl, of course I approve. Wholeheartedly. I was beginning to despair of you ever venturing out of this house again.'

'Father has been dead less than two months,' she reminded him, somewhat taken aback.

'That is no excuse for you to bury yourself here. You've cut yourself off from all your friends. It grieves me to see you so alone—because of me.'

'Dear Felipe, how thoughtful you are sometimes. Don't worry about me. I enjoy my daily rides . . .'

'Usually alone. Twice this week you have disobeyed me and ridden without protection.'

'I have not been near the Valle de Lágrimas in days and that is the only place I am likely to need it. Besides, with half our men guarding it, the remainder are trying to do the work of them all. We can spare no *vaqueros* to ride with me purely for pleasure.'

'That is true, but it does not stop me worrying about you when you go out alone, competent as you are. Still, from next week, things will be a little easier. Sancho is sending men to patrol the valley too. He is as concerned as we are that there should be no further unpleasant incidents . . .' Felipe broke off, frowning heavily as the servant refilling his wine glass spilt some on the snow-white cloth. Without moving from his chair, his hand flicked upwards and caught the man a stinging blow across the cheek. 'Clumsy idiot! The next time I will take a whip to you. Remove yourself and send in someone with a steady hand.'

'Felipe, it was an accident,' Ysanne protested. How she wished his moods would not change so swiftly. The momentary look in his eyes had been almost murderous—and over a drop of spilt wine!

'Do not tell me how to deal with the servants in my own house. Father was too lax with the idle devils. We give them everything they have, food, clothes, roofs over their heads and a living for the rest of their miserable lives. All I ask in return is that they do their duties well. I am a perfectionist, Ysanne. You, of all people, should know that by now.'

'Perfection is impossible, everyone has some flaw,' she returned with a half-smile.

'For most people, including you, my dear sister, I regret to say that is the truth. However, I know someone who does not have your shortcomings, or mine for that matter. When God created Manuela, he created perfection. That is why we are so suited to each other, don't you see? I am the only one who can truly appreciate her. I have to have her for that reason, if for no other.'

Ysanne felt herself grow very cold as she looked into her brother's smiling face. She knew he meant every word of what he said—and was afraid because of it. Afraid! Of her own brother? She was allowing her imagination to run wild again. He loved Manuela. No, worshipped her was nearer to the truth. The wildness of his youth, she was sure, was long past and what little remained could be curbed by the love of a woman. He was on edge, tense, and with good reason after what had happened lately or he would not have reacted so strongly to a simple accident.

'Now, what was I saying before I was so rudely interrupted?' He watched with narrowed gaze as another servant laid a napkin over the wine stain and proceeded to refill his glass without further mishap. Ysanne did not relax again until he had been dismissed and they were alone with their coffee. 'Ah, we were discussing Sancho. He is quite taken with you, did you know that? He has spoken to me of a deep and lasting attachment he hopes you may reciprocate.'

'That is out of the question,' Ysanne said quickly.

'Why? Because you are still in love with Ruy Valdez? The man responsible for our father's death.'

'No, I am not. I forbid you to speak of him.'

'Forbid?' Felipe savoured his brandy, watching her over the rim of the glass. 'Surely it should not be necessary to remind you that I am master here— Father left everything to me as his son and legal heir. You are not yet of age, Ysanne, and therefore subject to my protection. He would have wished it to be so, you know that. Your disastrous—almost disastrous—alliance with Ruy has brought you nothing but pain and unhappiness. If a man like Sancho Morales, a powerful and influential figure in this part of the country, looks on you with favour, I should respond well. Lose him and you might well end up an old maid. You are nearly twenty, a woman in the full bloom of her youth. You should have a husband and children by now.'

'I have already told you I shall never marry. Felipe, be reasonable. You have no idea what you are asking of me. It is impossible,' she pleaded, her expression growing distraught. Was it his intention to marry her off to Sancho? 'I thought you were glad I had come home, that we are close again. These past few weeks we have learned to know each other again—and now you want to be rid of me.'

'Nothing of the kind. I want you to be happy. It would be a good marriage. The Morales name, plus his powerful friends in high places, could be useful to us in our fight against Pinos Altos. If we are to survive, we must consider every possibility. I have told Sancho he has my permission to speak to you.'

'That—that is unforgivable,' Ysanne gasped, rising to her feet. 'I will not be a pawn, Felipe, so that you can have your revenge on Ruy.'

'The man you no longer love.' The sarcasm in his voice brought the colour surging into her cheeks and she turned towards the door in confusion. 'Sancho spoke of his feelings for you to Father a few weeks before he died. You were the real reason he has been coming to this house all these years. Who do you think our father would prefer to see you wed, Ysanne? A man who cares for you, or a man who would use you in his struggle for power? Break your heart and then, most likely, toss you out to fend for yourself? I hope you speak the truth when you say no longer love Ruy because I have sworn an oath that one day I will bring him to account for what he has done. I am going to kill him. I have invited Sancho to lunch with us tomorrow. Think carefully on what I have said. I would be displeased if you were impolite to him after the exceptional kindness he has shown to you.'

'Doña Ysanne, have I said anything to offend you? Throughout lunch you were very quiet and you looked so sad.' Sancho Morales laid a hand on Ysanne's arm and drew her to a halt as they walked together in the gardens. She knew Felipe was watching them from the upstairs verandah where he lounged in a chair with coffee and brandy. Serafina followed at a respectful distance behind them, her expression betraying the fact she did not know what to make of this new alliance.

'Of course not. Forgive my preoccupation with

other thoughts,' she answered, forcing a smile to her lips as she turned to face him.

'Pleasant ones, I hope, although from the look I saw in your eyes earlier I rather doubt it. Do you have some problem you cannot confide to your brother? Something I could help with perhaps?'

Ysanne's heart warmed towards him. It was not his fault she could not look on him as anything more than a friend. She hesitated for a moment only before replying.

'Regretfully, Don Sancho, I must tell you my problem is you!'

'*Dios!* What have I done?' He stepped back from her with a concerned expression and she was aware of Felipe leaning forward to watch them more intently.

'Let us walk in the shade of the trees,' she said and, linking her arm through his, drew him beneath the leafy coolness of the three trees in the centre of the garden, whose branches intertwined over a wrought-iron seat. 'I am the one at fault,' she hastened to add as they sat down.

'In what way?' Sancho's level gaze studied her. Somehow it gave her the confidence she needed to explain her position openly and honestly.

'You have spoken to my brother, have you not? About me?'

'*Sí*. This distresses you? The fact I want you for my wife?' He sounded quite amazed, Ysanne thought, as if he had not considered a refusal to his proposition possible. 'I spoke to your father also, but his untimely death deprived me of his answer.'

'It would have been no. He knew I loved another man.'

'Ruy Valdez?'

'I have told my brother I no longer love Ruy. He would not understand my feelings and I do not wish him to be hurt further, but it is only fair you should know the truth. I will never love another man until the day I die, nor will I marry and spend the rest of my life living a lie.'

She raised a hand to smooth back a strand of hair freed by a strong breeze, and he saw it was trembling. He caught her fingers and touched them to his lips.

'When you have reached my age, Ysanne, you will have discovered there are different kinds of love. I will never feel the same kind of turbulent passion that I experienced with my first wife. We were married young and we enjoyed our years together. It takes many years to grow to know someone. Unbridled passions of spring blossom into the rich maturity of summer and then mellow into the golden days of autumn. And winter? Winter is spent in the afterglow of all those wonderful years, full of memories.'

'How can you think of marrying again, having loved her so?'

'I am a lonely man. I have a fine house, but only myself to talk to. Most of the rooms have been closed since she died. They are as silent and unfulfilled as I now am. I want to hear the sound of a woman's voice again, hear her laughter, the excited, noisy chatter of children . . .' He broke off as Ysanne's hand grew tense in his. 'Yes, I want a family. It is my dearest wish. I would ask for no greater honour than that you become my wife and fulfill the last of my hopes—my dreams.'

'What—what you ask is impossible,' Ysanne stammered. His quiet conviction was almost frightening. He still expected her to consider his offer, she was sure. He had not listened to a word she said.

'Because you are unwilling to commit yourself to the bed of a man you do not love?' he challenged and his words brought bright colour to her cheeks. 'Come now, I am sure I do not shock you,' he chided, not unkindly. 'It is the truth, is it not?' She nodded, not answering. To lie in any arms other than those of the man she loved was unthinkable! 'Patience also comes with time and I am a very patient man, Ysanne. I believe you when you say you still love Ruy. I understand too, the terrible grief and agony of mind you must have endured since your father died. I will not dwell on it on such a lovely day. Be my wife! Give your life some meaning. Let me try to replace a little of the love you have lost.'

'Don Sancho—I am not worthy of such consideration!' Bright tears sparkled in Ysanne's eyes.

'Think on it. I will not accept an answer now. I have your brother's permission to call whenever I wish, but I will not do so if you ask me not to.'

'I shall be pleased to see you again—as my friend.'

'*Bueno*. Now I must take my leave of you. No, wait, I have forgotten something.' From his pocket he produced a small leather box and pressed it into her hands. 'A rather belated homecoming present.'

Ysanne found herself staring at a large sapphire ring, set in gold. She swallowed hard, snapped shut the lid and held it out to him. There was no doubt in her mind it had originally been intended as a betrothal ring!

'You have misunderstood,' Sancho said with a sigh. He made no attempt to take it back.

'No, señor, you did, with Felipe's help. He too, would like to see this match agreed.'

'He has become a sensible young man of late. Responsibility suits him.' The ring was taken from the box and slipped on to her right hand. 'You are quite correct in assuming it was meant for another purpose, but as you have made it quite plain you consider that out of the question, momentarily anyway, please accept this simply as a gift, accompanied by my deepest affection. Should you reconsider your position, I shall know when I see it on the correct finger.'

'I cannot accept it under such conditions,' Ysanne protested.

'Let us continue the discussion the next time we are together, shall we? *Adiós, mi niña.* Think of me a little until we meet again.'

'I shall think of you every time I look at my lovely—present, Don Sancho,' she said meaningly.

'That, at least, is a beginning.'

Watching his carriage roll out through the main gates, Ysanne felt as if she had come up against an unsurmountable object, yet she could not dislike him—and that fact she found more disturbing than anything else.

As the days passed Ysanne knew she was being carefully cultivated by Sancho in order to look upon his marriage proposal more favourably. She tried hard not to do so, but there was no faulting his impeccable conduct, and his genuine desire to please her was apparent to everyone in the *quinta*. Serafina went so far as to remark that it was too good an offer to refuse and earned herself a sharp rebuke for her thoughtless tongue.

Marriage was out of the question, she told Sancho with firm determination the next time he came to call. In return she received a lecture on how lonely she would be alone, without love, her life without purpose.

Without purpose! The words lingered with her long after they had parted. Was the only purpose of a woman's life to marry and bear children? She had wanted it once, but it had been denied her. She would now find other things to fill the emptiness within her. She was needed at the *hacienda*; Felipe could not manage it alone. The *vaqueros* and their families too needed her for they looked to her to give fair judgment when her brother's desire for perfection made a routine day almost unbearable for each and every one of them.

She had finished breakfast and was on her way upstairs to change and go riding, when angry voices coming from the *sala* slowed her steps. Instinctively she knew something was wrong as Felipe emerged with García, the head *vaquero*. He had served her father long and faithfully for more than ten years and she had never known a harsh word pass between them, but since Felipe had taken over the relationship had been stormy and precarious. She had first put it down to a clash of personalities. An older, more knowledgeable man resenting the intrusion of a younger, inexperienced man into a world he knew little about. However, of late she had begun to change her mind. Daily she learned from Serafina of the growing discontent among the *peónes* and tenants. Felipe was pushing them too hard. In an effort to prove himself, she suspected, but even so, it was too hard and too quickly and they resented it. She would have to speak to him, tactfully of course. She knew he would neither expect nor welcome criticism from her.

'What is it, Felipe?'

'More trouble. *Dios*, I thought it was over, that your return had made him think twice about continuing with his mad schemes. Now it begins again,' Felipe snapped. His face was taut with rage. Eyes glittering he stepped towards her. 'Early this morning García took some men to relieve those at the waterhole. He found them all dead and thirty head of our cattle slaughtered. Go and change. I want you to see this for yourself. It's time you understood the kind of animal I am fighting.'

Stunned, Ysanne obeyed him. Men and cattle slaughtered! She too, had begun to think the violence was over for there had been none since the death of her father. No name had passed between them, but she knew they were both thinking of the same man. She had not seen Ruy Valdez since the funeral, nor heard from him. Not even one short note—a word in his own defence! Her confession of love had meant nothing at all to him. She was a fool to hope for a non-existent miracle to happen which would prove his innocence.

Felipe watched her as she emerged from the house and his narrowed gaze centred on the white silk blouse she wore, open at the neck, the tight-fitting leather trousers and leather boots. She took the reins of her horse from the waiting *vaquero* and swung herself into the saddle with an easy grace which made him inwardly wince. She did everything so well. This was the old Ysanne, the girl who rode like a man and revelled in the fact. Had worked alongside the *peónes* and women in the fields in time of hardship for the ranch, had taken his place at his father's side, more knowledgeable in the way it was run than he would ever be. Capable—independent—everything he was not.

At that moment Felipe realised how much he had always hated her.

CHAPTER FIVE

YSANNE took one look into her brother's closed face as they rode away and refrained from pressing him with questions. The waterhole which served all three estates was on the last of the low ground before it began to rise towards the slopes of the Sierra Nevada mountains. Only once, when she was seven years old, did Ysanne remember it being dry. That was after three years of continual drought. It was a natural lake fed by underground streams from the granite peaks towering in the distance. Twice it had been enlarged by her father to accommodate torrents of water which poured into it either through an excess of rainfall or a prolonged summer, which melted more snow than usual from the mountain tops.

Silver birch glistened in the distance, intermingled with dark green willowy firs and pines, sometimes so tall they seemed to disappear into the fleecy white clouds passing overhead.

As a child she had swum here with Juan and Ruy, a tomboy, reckless and uninhibited. The three of them had shared many happy hours together, riding, swimming, exploring the countryside around Pinos Altos. She had never been afraid in their company. Juan was a good tracker and Ruy an excellent shot, with a second sense for danger which had averted trouble for them on more than one occasion. The day they had found a stray cougar cub and been attacked by its mother would forever remain clear in her memory. Ruy had stepped between her and the enraged animal and managed to stun it with his rifle, rather than kill it and deprive the cub of its mother. His shoulder still bore the scars of that encounter. That was the Ruy she loved—not the stranger she had encountered on her return home.

The stench of death which hung about the waterhole had already begun to attract hungry buzzards. Ysanne shivered as she watched them circling in the sky overhead and Felipe looked at her with an annoyed frown. She had been steeling herself to remain composed. Even so, nausea rose in her stomach at the scene before her eyes. The cattle had been shot where they stood, many beside the shallows of the lake as they drank from the cool water. A few, probably frightened by the noise of gun-fire, had turned and run, but they had not gone more than twenty yards before they too died.

One of the guards lay sprawled on the ground. Another was half-resting in a sitting position against some rocks, his rifle by his side, apparently untouched. As if the person, or persons who approached him were known to him—even friends, she thought. She counted another four motionless figures, some had been shot from behind. Six good men murdered! There would be many tears shed tonight among the villagers.

'It is too horrible,' she breathed, raising stricken eyes to those of her brother as she drew rein beside him. 'Why—how could Ruy have been involved in such a massacre of innocent people?'

'It is my belief he wishes to push us into open

warfare. We would be at a disadvantage, Ysanne. The house is on open ground, unprotected, while he lives in the high country, with men guarding every trail, no doubt. Think how easy it would be for him to keep us from this waterhole, if he chose. His men could sit for weeks on those slopes, months even, and attack us at will. More men lost. More cattle butchered. To reach the town we have to ride through the valley, that means taking men from the house, leaving it virtually unprotected, unless Sancho gives us extra support. We dare not risk using the back trail. There are a hundred places for men to hide and ambush us and it takes two extra days. I think today Ruy is flexing his muscles, showing us what he is capable of doing if he chooses.'

'Did you speak to the sheriff again?' Ysanne interrupted. 'Have there been strangers in the town lately, or have you or Sancho dismissed any men who might want revenge and seek this callous way of having it?'

'So you still look for an alternative explanation. You disappoint me,' Felipe snapped, his expression hardening. 'More than that, you disgust me! If he came to you now and told you a pack of lies you would believe them, because you are still in love with him.'

'No!'

'Liar! Your face betrays you, every time his name is mentioned. Mark my words this will happen again and again unless he is stopped.'

'How do you propose to do that?' she asked stiffly. 'We had men patrolling the valley, yet this still happened.'

'By fighting fire with fire.' He turned to the silent

vaquero at his side. 'García, show my sister who else you found here.'

The order was obeyed with a sullen gesture which implied to Ysanne it was against the man's better judgment. Dismounting he strode to a clump of mesquite bushes and dragged into view the body of a boy in his early teens. She caught her breath as she saw the intricately woven belt he wore. An indian! For years, since the death of Ruy's mother, there had been indians employed at Pinos Altos, mostly Navajos. Ruy himself had been raised by a Navajo woman and had given one the important position as foreman after his father's death, so Felipe had told her. His childhood friend, Chato, she suspected. She remembered the tall, stoic-faced man well. He had idolised Ruy from the day he set foot in the house and there were times she had even thought he resented her close friendship with the two brothers.

'Tell me now Ruy Valdez was not behind this outrage?' her brother demanded and her face was desolate in her defeat.

'I cannot—this is one of his men. Felipe, before you make rash accusations, be sure. Perhaps he no longer worked there. This could have been the work of some renegade band, it has happened before.' But she knew she was clutching at straws so that she would not have totally to condemn him.

'Go back to the house, you are of no use to me here. Unless you pull yourself together, Ysanne, I am beginning to think it will be best if you return to Monterey. You no longer feel for the ranch or our land as you did before. I am prepared to fight to keep what is ours. All you can do is dwell on what might have been—with him! *Dios*, the sooner I free you from him the better for us all. Go home. I have work to do.'

Without a word Ysanne turned her horse about, acutely conscious of having disgraced herself before all the watching *vaqueros*. Each day she resolved to be more steadfast in her support of her brother, her condemnation of the man who had set on a deliberate course to destroy them, but when it was demanded she make a stand and voice that condemnation before everyone, she failed miserably.

She heard Felipe issuing orders behind her, heard horses gallop swiftly away, but dared not look back. Where was he going? Surely not to Pinos Altos to confront Ruy? Not with a dozen men?

Upon her return to the house she would break the news of the massacre to the unsuspecting families and then spend the remainder of the time until Felipe returned in contemplation of the awful facts she had refused to accept totally until today. When she faced him again it would be as the sister prepared to support him under any circumstances. Total commitment. There was no question of her returning to her aunt in Monterey. It was time to stop thinking of herself and consider her brother, remember all those brave promises she made to him when their father died. To stand by him and be his strength as he had been hers!

You have the heart of a lion and the bearing of a queen, he had told her at the graveside. He had given her courage when she needed it desperately. Now she must do the same for him. He was at times irresponsible, headstrong. He had become increasingly moody since the death of their father, plagued by doubts. Not only the ranch would suffer if they did not work together, but their own newly-found relationship would wither and die before it had a real chance to mature.

She became aware of the sound of drumming hoofs behind her and at once slowed her horse to look around, expecting to find that Felipe had sent one of the men to escort her home. Her eyes narrowed against the glare of the sun which momentarily blinded her. Out of the brilliance came two horsemen, blurred against the shimmering heat haze. Only when they were close was she able to see them clearly and then she stiffened in the saddle with shock as she recognised the white stocking bay one of them was riding.

Ruy Valdez had followed it for four weeks in the high country the summer before she went away, until he finally trapped it in a rocky valley. He had spent another month coaxing it to accept him, sitting with it for hours, talking quietly, soothingly, as it stood tethered to a tree a few feet away. At no time had he used a whip or force of any kind to make the animal accept him. At the end of four weeks, it obeyed him implicitly, would even eat out of his hand. Wild stallion and man had merged into one, Ysanne remembered thinking as she watched them together. Such trust and patience. Such understanding, almost love between them.

She hesitated for a moment only before digging her heels into her horse's flanks. It was a fast mount, perhaps it could outrun the bay, but deep in her heart she knew it could not. She was easily outdistanced. Ruy reined in directly in her path, forcing her to do likewise to avoid a collision. Instantly her reins were seized, thrown to the waiting Juan and she was dragged unceremoniously to the ground. She fought against his hold like a wildcat, but in the end had to submit to his greater strength and suffer the indignity of his touch.

'Why did you run?' he demanded angrily. 'You recognised us.'

'What better reason,' she retorted throwing back her head to look at him. Eyes as brilliant as emeralds burned with fire as they stared at him. She must not weaken in her resolve! What she felt for him was dead— as her father was dead!

'I've been waiting for two weeks for you to ride this way.'

'We have nothing to say to each other. When I wanted you, prayed for you to come, you did not! You are everything Felipe says you are.'

Attack, attack, her determined mind dictated. Listen, oh listen, her heart entreated. Look at his face! Your words have hurt him.

'What am I, Ysanne?' He shook her slightly. 'What do you think I am? Have you been conditioned yet or are you still capable of thinking for yourself?'

'Power hungry, that is what you are. You want the Valle de Lágrimas,' she cried. To her horror and puzzlement he laughed outright in her face.

'If I wanted it—if—I could take it now and hold it against your brother and Sancho Morales. The two of you combined cannot combat the strength of Pinos Altos.'

'Then—then you admit it,' she whispered, appalled.

He shook her again, harder this time, and the ribbon slipped from her hair, sending red-gold curls swinging free about her shoulders.

'I said if. I don't want your land.' His tone was contemptuous.

'Then why did you kill my father?'

The blow he dealt her sent Ysanne reeling backwards into Juan's arms. She heard the young man's voice raised in protest as she struggled to compose herself.

'Ysanne . . .' His arms were gentle about her shoulders, on the soft skin already bruised by Ruy's fierce grip. 'You do not understand. Please listen to him before it is too late.'

'You too?' She wrenched herself free, eyes flaming. 'I have seen for myself, not an hour ago, what lengths you will go to. Men killed, cattle butchered. Dear heaven, your reasoning is beyond me . . .'

'What men? What cattle?' Ruy and Juan spoke almost simultaneously and she had to force herself over the inclination to believe the incredulity in their voices.

'At the waterhole.'

'But our cattle are there too,' Juan interposed.

'No, there are only cattle from our ranch. Dead animals and dead men. Good men—and one who, I believe, belongs at Pinos Altos. All the proof my brother needed that the men who committed the outrage were sent by you.'

'That means they are either dead too or scattered over half the countryside like the last lot we lost there,' Ruy muttered grimly. 'I must go back. You go on to town and bring Manuela home. I don't want her riding out here alone. I will go back to the waterhole.'

'If Felipe is there he will kill you,' Ysanne breathed.

'Only if my back is turned,' came the derisive

retort. 'Go now, Juan and stay with her if I am not at the *rancho* when you return. Post guards on all the trails too, just to make sure we do not have unwelcome visitors.'

'We will be back before nightfall. *Adiós*, Ysanne. *Vaya con Dios*,' Juan said quietly as he backed towards his horse. He gave her the impression he wanted to stay.

As she watched him ride away she was again plagued with doubts that he, who had always been quiet and shy, could have accused her brother of the murder of Don Pedro. Had, in fact, become as violent and unpredictable as his elder brother. To believe otherwise meant Felipe was a liar, a schemer beyond her wildest imagination. That too had to be dismissed. Had Ruy not assaulted him that day in the study after striking down her father? Had Felipe not gone out of his way to give her her freedom if she wished it? Had she not seen with her own eyes how someone was out to destroy the Hacienda de las Flores?

She turned to mount, but Ruy's fingers fastened around her wrist in an iron grip.

'Not yet, *chica*. You and I are going to talk without Felipe's beady little eyes on us. There will be truth between us now. Why did you not answer my letter?'

'Letters? What letters? I have received nothing from you.'

He swore under his breath.

'*Dios!* Felipe!'

'Let me go. We have nothing to say to each other.' She must not allow him to see how afraid she was of his touch, his nearness. These things could destroy her.

'Not even after that very pretty speech you made at the graveside of your father?' he mocked. 'I must admit you shattered me with such a touching confession, but that was the idea, was it not? To gain sympathy before all your friends? Whose idea was it, by the way—Felipe's or yours?'

'You are nothing to me.' She spat the words at him. He thought it had been pure fabrication! Her first impulse to deny such a monstrous accusation died on her lips as she saw the advantage of remaining silent. Let him think the worst of her if it kept a barrier erected between them.

'*Sí*, that is what I thought. When your father talked of a match between us I told him it was not possible,' Ruy declared, his mouth twisting sardonically and she stopped fighting against his hold and stared at him in wide-eyed disbelief. 'I told him you had already found someone in Monterey with your aunt's help, I suspect. He chose to ignore my words.'

'He—he spoke of marriage—to you! When?'

'Months ago. The day you came home I was on my way to give him my answer.'

'Doubtless during that time you had come to realise the advantages of being married to the daughter of Don Diego de Rivas. The possibilities of merging the two estates into one when he died and left the place to me . . .' She broke off as Ruy's eyes narrowed sharply. She had told no one of the plans her father had made to provide for her after his death, not even Serafina, and it was clear from the way Felipe had accepted the will leaving it to him, that he had never considered it might have been any other way.

Her father had spoken of it the night before she

left, of his determination that all her loyalty and hard work done in her brother's place would not go unrewarded. There would be a new will, he had told her, in her favour. She protested at this. She had the Valle de Lágrimas, it was sufficient, but he was adamant. Upon his death she would inherit everything.

She had not, but she had remained silent, quite content with what she already had and pleased that her father had found Felipe worthy of continuing in his stead.

'You knew,' she accused. 'I can see it in your face. He told you that too! Now I understand so many things . . .'

'He mentioned it. He wanted to be sure you would be taken care of in every way. Damn you, girl, have you lost all sense of reason? He did not want to give everything to Felipe because he knew it would only increase his overwhelming lust for power.'

'He thinks the same of you.'

'And you believe him?'

'I believe the evidence of my own eyes.'

'As I do.' He was looking down at the ring on her finger and his eyes were suddenly cold and unfriendly. 'It is true, then, what Felipe has been telling everyone? You are betrothed to Sancho.'

'No, I mean . . . there is nothing settled,' she stammered, her mind beginning to reel again under this new shock. What had Felipe been telling people behind her back and why was he so anxious to push her into a marriage he knew was not to her liking?

'Only the ring,' Ruy drawled and the contempt in his tone brought fierce colour to her cheeks. The barrier between them was steadily growing higher. It was what she wanted and yet would have given anything to destroy! 'My congratulations, he is a fortunate *hombre*—and you are a fool. Is that all you want out of life, *chica*? To share the bed of an old man so that he can have a family before he dies?'

The insult robbed her of speech and then she swung back her hand to hit him in indignation. He easily averted the blow and coupled both her wrists in one lean hand.

'A little fire at last. Now that is the Ysanne I used to know. What a waste! He is not man enough to tame you . . .'

'No more are you.'

'The last time you issued a challenge I tossed you into the waterhole until you cooled down,' he said amusedly, but the dark eyes considering her were full of shadows and she felt herself begin to tremble.

Spurred on by his taunts to reckless action, she bent her head and sank her teeth into the back of his hand. He did not release her as she hoped. Instead, fastening his free hand in her loose cloud of hair, he jerked back her head and stared down into her scarlet cheeks.

'This is to remember me by until we meet again, my little wildcat. Sancho will never have you. I gave your father my word and I will keep it, although it is no longer to my liking—or yours, it seems,' he scathed, and his mouth descended without warning on hers, taking it by storm, rendering her immobile—unable to think or protest in any way at this final, humiliating insult.

Her lips were cold and stiff, refusing to yield to

his silent demand to surrender herself to his domination, but she was totally unprepared for the shattering of her defences which that long drawn out kiss brought about.

She felt herself weakening in his embrace, felt tears scald her cheeks, her mouth, as with a soft moan of utter despair her lips parted beneath his. For a long moment he held her, then her tears touched his lips and he drew back with a startled oath. As his hands fell away from her, Ysanne ran to her horse. She heard him call her name again and again as she raced away from the shame of her surrender, the knowledge she would always love him—no matter what!

She remembered nothing of the ride home, blinded by tears. She ran past startled servants into the house, ignoring the questioning looks directed after her as they gazed at her lathered horse, to throw herself across the bed in the sanctuary of her room and allow the full floodtide of tears to flow unsuppressed. When at last they receded, she fell asleep where she lay. Exhausted in mind and body.

She was roused by Serafina gently shaking her shoulder. Somehow she roused herself from the sleep that had unexpectedly claimed her. Her head ached and her mouth was as dry as dust. One look at her swollen cheeks sent the woman hurrying to fetch water from the porcelain pitcher on the dresser.

'You have a visitor,' Serafina said. 'Be still now and let me bathe away this redness. *Santa María*, what a state you are in, and it's no wonder after what he made you see this morning. Why didn't you send for me, I was only with old Adelina? She lost her grandson out there, Anna María, her husband. Poor lamb and her only married a month.'

'Who—who told our people?'

'García. They knew before your brother. They do not like what is happening, *mi niña*. There is talk of leaving here and finding work at another *rancho*. One that does not have a cloud of death hovering over it.'

'Don't talk like that.' Ysanne sat up, raising a hand to her throbbing temples. Her skin was burning like fire. 'Did you say something about a visitor?'

'Señorita Casale has been waiting almost half an hour.'

'Manuela here! To see me, or Felipe?' Perhaps she had come in answer to Felipe's prayers.

'He has not yet returned. She asked only for you.'

'Good heavens, what a mess I look!' Ysanne declared, staring down at her creased blouse. 'But I cannot keep her waiting any longer. Just do something with my hair.'

'The señorita did ask if Don Felipe was at home,' Serafina added as she deftly wielded a brush on her mistress' dishevelled hair. 'There, that is more presentable. She gave me the impression she would not have remained had he been here.'

Which was very out of character for the girl Felipe vehemently claimed to return his passionate feelings and was being forced to marry another man against her will, Ysanne thought as she went downstairs to greet the unexpected arrival.

Manuela Casale rose from a chair to greet her as she entered the drawing-room, pleasantly cool now that the shutters had been closed against the heat of the midday sun. Her pretty face was pale and strained, Ysanne saw, and the hands which clasped hers trembled visibly.

She was a pretty girl, almost nineteen now, with large, expressive blue eyes and a pleasant way about her that had always made her the most popular girl for many miles, Ysanne remembered. She wore a plain blue riding outfit which did credit to a neat figure, with a small hat in a matching colour perched on a shining chignon of brown hair.

'Manuela, how nice to see you,' she said as she lightly brushed a kiss on each cheek. It was the truth. She had no quarrel with this girl. They had not been close friends in the past, but had shared an amicable relationship which she saw no reason to discontinue because of what was happening. She could have no part in the schemes being laid at Pinos Altos. If anything, she was as much a pawn in the game being played as Ysanne herself!

'Are you really? I was so afraid you would not want to see me. When you did not come down . . . I was on the point of leaving, before . . . before Felipe came back,' Manuela said, relief flooding into her tone. 'I was on my way home from town and I thought this would be an ideal opportunity to see you and talk, but I must not stay too long or Ruy will send someone looking for me and that could cause more bad feeling between us all.'

'Is Juan not with you?' Ysanne asked in puzzlement. 'I saw him this morning, on his way to town to collect you.'

'Oh, dear! I rode the back trail which skirts the valley to avoid any of Ruy's *vaqueros* seeing me. He has given orders I am not to roam the countryside alone. He is so afraid for me. He says little, but I know he fears for us all.'

'Perhaps he is afraid you may learn the truth.' Ysanne moved away from her to perch herself on the arm of a chair. 'Sit down, Manuela. If we have only a little while together, let us make the most of it.'

'Felipe . . .' the girl began.

'Why do you say his name as if you have something to fear from him?' Ysanne demanded, frowning at the tenseness about the girl which could not be controlled even in her presence. 'You know he loves you. Adores you! If you had only heard the way he spoke of you to me. Your marriage to Juan will break him.'

'You don't know what you are saying,' Manuela said shrilly, clasping her hands tightly together in her lap. 'I knew you didn't. He has lied to you as he has everyone else! I do not love him, Ysanne. I never have, nor ever will give him the slightest encouragement to think otherwise. In fact I—I cannot stand to be near him! Forgive me, but it is the truth. He terrifies me. The ways he looks at me, talks at me, not to me, as if I was some possession he had just acquired . . .'

'He loves you,' Ysanne repeated. 'He thinks you are perfection itself. "When God created Manuela, he created perfection. That is why we are so suited to each other".' Her voice trailed off as she remembered Felipe's words to her as they sat at dinner and once again, she felt herself grow cold with a fear she did not understand. 'Why should he tell everyone you return his feelings if you do not?' Why had he spread the rumour she was engaged to Sancho when it was not true? That question would have to wait. Others that had been clamouring at her brain for weeks might now be answered. 'Were you not secretly planning to marry my brother when Don Pedro had his accident?'

'No! No!' There were tears of genuine distress in the girl's eyes. 'When—when his attentions became too demanding, I begged him to leave me alone. I told him I was in love with Juan, that I had spoken to Ruy, who I hoped would in turn speak to his father and allow us to marry. He would not accept it. He talked so strangely. Of being the only one who could ever truly appreciate me, that no one else was good enough. In desperation I told Ruy how pressing he had become. He spoke to Don Pedro and after that, for a while at least, nothing happened. And then I was suddenly being congratulated by my friends on my forthcoming marriage to Felipe. He was telling everyone it was all arranged. Don Pedro immediately announced my betrothal to Juan to counteract his ridiculous story. Instead of congratulations, I then received words of sympathy—pity, because Don Pedro had decided his son was a better match for the daughter of his oldest friend. For weeks I did not go near the town. I could not bear any more questions and I was so terribly afraid I would meet Felipe. Juan had sworn to have it out with him in public, make him admit his story was a lie. They did meet one day. It was horrible. Felipe refused to fight, but he was so rude and provocative, Juan struck the first blow—and many more. If Ruy had not intervened . . .' Manuela hid her face in her hands and was silent for a long while. Ysanne sat like a statue. There was more she knew. She had to know everything!

'Has Ruy spoken of what happened here the

day my father died?' she managed to ask at long length.

Manuela produced a lace-edged handkerchief from her purse and dabbed dry her eyes.

'No. Not even to Juan. We both saw him come home, riding like the wind and his face . . . I have never seen such an expression before. It was as if he had been given the world and lost it in the same moment. He did not go to bed that night. Chato said he drank a whole bottle of brandy sitting alone on the verandah. I know Juan has asked him what happened, but he has said nothing.'

'The brandy no doubt alleviated the voice of his conscience.'

'I do not believe he attacked your father, Ysanne.'

'Felipe was there. He saw it, and afterwards he himself was attacked,' Ysanne said.

'And you believe him? The word of a proven liar?' Manuela's words hung in the air between them. They brought Ysanne to her feet, eyes flashing angrily.

'He is my brother. Your word against his. Who would you expect me to believe?'

'Blind faith, Ysanne. Open your eyes before it is too late for us all. Come to Pinos Altos! Talk to Ruy . . .'

'That is not possible,' she returned coldly.

'Are you so afraid we are all speaking the truth?' Manuela demanded, her young face growing indignant. 'Where is the love you proclaimed before everyone?'

'Dead—like my father.'

'Did it ever exist? Perhaps it was only a figment of your imagination, as my love for Felipe is only in his mind. Do you think alike, Ysanne? I pity you if you do . . .'

'Please, go!' Ysanne strode to the door and flung it open, her face an ashen mask of indecision. 'No, wait! I will ride with you until you are within sight of the boundaries of Pinos Altos. After what happened today it will be safer for you.'

'That will not be necessary,' Manuela said, drawing on her riding gloves. Ysanne's rebuff had clearly hurt her. 'I was a fool to come, wasn't I?'

'You meant well.' Ysanne's tone softened slightly. Manuela was in love and love clouded the vision. She could testify to that. 'There was trouble at the waterhole this morning. We lost many cattle and six men were killed. The mood of the villagers may not be too friendly if they see you leave here alone.

Ysanne did indeed notice the hostile glances directed at her companion as they emerged into the sweltering heat of the afternoon sun, but the only comment uttered was not taken up by the rest of the onlookers as she turned and fixed the man responsible with a withering look. She saw it was the brother of Anna María, the young bride of only a month who had lost her husband and she refrained from a verbal warning. Restraint was needed, not more fuel poured on already troubled waters.

They had been riding for some ten minutes and were barely out of the orange groves which stretched for some two miles alongside the *hacienda*, when Juan Valdez was alongside them. To Ysanne's relief he was alone, probably on his way back from the town after finding Manuela had already left. At least, she hoped so.

'What were you doing at the de Rivas ranch?' he demanded of the girl. 'Ruy expressly forbade you to go there. He also told you to wait in town until one of us came to escort you home.'

'Don't be angry, Juan, I felt I had to see Ysanne and try to explain.' Manuela shrugged her slim shoulders. 'She would not listen, even for Ruy's sake. Please take me home.'

'Wait,' Ysanne said with a frown. 'How did you know she was at the ranch?'

'I picked up her tracks when she turned off in the valley. My father often used to come the same way when he visited Don Diego. Perhaps you didn't know that?'

'No. Why should I? I always ride through the valley. I enjoy it more that way.'

'And of course you were away when he died. When Ruy and I found him that morning there was another set of tracks beside his body. Those of a single horse and they led back here to the house. I should know, I followed them.' Juan's gaze centred on her pale face, his young mouth tightening into a bleak line. 'I brought the sheriff here to show him, but by then they had been obliterated. No one saw them but Ruy—and me.'

'How convenient,' Ysanne said and his sunburnt features darkened.

'Ruy is right, you have changed.' He swung his horse about. 'Let's go home, Manuela.'

'Juan—I will come to Pinos Altos. I will talk with Ruy, the day after tomorrow.' The words tumbled from Ysanne's lips, faltering, but uttered.

He spun around in the saddle, searching her face with suspicious eyes.

'You mean it? Just you?'

'*Sí*. Let Ruy convince me of his innocence if he can. I will listen, but I promise nothing.'

'Oh, Ysanne, it is all he has been hoping for,' Manuela breathed. 'You will not regret it.'

But as she rode homewards, Ysanne realised she was already regretting the impulsive gesture which would take her into the high country, to Pinos Altos, the domain of Ruy Valdez. Her brother's sworn enemy—the man she had accused of murder. How would she be received after their encounter that morning? Would she be received at all?

CHAPTER SIX

'No, none of these is really suitable,' Ysanne said, looking up from the letter she was trying to write to contemplate the three dresses Serafina was holding out for her inspection. The woman returned them to the closet with a sigh. 'The green velvet was not too bad, was it? I will look at it again when I have finished this letter to Don Sancho. I am not going to marry him. He must accept it once and for all. So must Felipe. I shall never marry.' Serafina silently cursed the man who had turned her mistress into someone only half alive. 'By the way, I shall be riding early tomorrow morning. Tell Pablito I want my horse saddled by seven o'clock.'

She decided it would be best to leave the house before Felipe roused himself, which was not usually before nine o'clock. By the time he had breakfasted and begun to wonder where she was, she would have reached the Valdez lands and could not be brought back. Time and time again she had balked at the decision she had so rashly made. It was madness! Stupidity! Disloyalty to her brother. But she had promised to go to Pinos Altos and she would go, in the hope of discovering the truth.

Manuela had spoken so forcefully in Ruy's defence, yet even she had admitted she knew nothing of what had taken place the day her father died to bring Ruy home in murderous mood, forsaking her company and that of his brother, to sit alone and drink. Had Chato shared the anguish of his thoughts that night, she wondered? Had Ruy unburdened the dark deeds locked in his soul to the only man whose intense loyalty and devotion decreed he would never judge his actions, never betray him?

'There, it is done.' Some while later she folded two pieces of paper and slipped them into an envelope, carefully sealing it. Her head still ached abominably.

The sitting-room seemed unusually stuffy and oppressive, although it was late afternoon and should have been considerably cooler than it was. There would be a storm tonight, she thought, to interrupt her badly needed sleep. The sound of thunder would do nothing to soothe her jangled nerves. Usually she liked to watch the lightning from the verandah and listen to the great booming sound of the thunder as it reverberated up and down the Valle de Lágrimas. When she had been a little girl and afraid of the noise, Serafina had bounced her on plump knees and told her how God and his angels were celebrating on account of another poor sinner repenting and being admitted to the Kingdom of Heaven.

Ysanne turned her attention to the addressing of the envelope for a moment, her brows drawn together in fierce concentration. It had not been an easy letter to write. She had asked Sancho to come to dinner the next Saturday. It was her intention then to tell him quite firmly and definitely that she was not going to marry him. She would return his ring too, so that no misunderstandings arose in the future between them. She dearly hoped he would remain her staunch friend and continue to visit her at the house. If all did not go well when she saw Ruy, she would be in desperate need of his friendship and the support she would be forced to ask for in order to protect her home and lands.

'Is my brother home yet?'

'*Sí*, a few minutes ago. He went directly to his room. I would not trouble him now,' she added as Ysanne rose and turned towards the door. 'He—he looked tired. Perhaps he means to rest for a while.'

'He is eating in town with Don Sancho. He will be going out again very soon. I don't want him to leave without my letter.'

Tired was not the first impression which leapt to Ysanne's mind as she knocked on her brother's door and slipped quickly inside. He was not there and the whole room screamed of chaos. On the floor at her feet lay a dusty jacket, torn in places. Beyond that, the white scarf he always wore around his neck. She froze in horror at the sight of the blood-spattered shirt which had been tossed over a chair near the doorway leading to his dressing-room. She could hear the sound of water being splashed into a bowl. On feet of lead she moved forward, not knowing what to expect.

Stripped to the waist, Felipe was drying himself with a towel. In silence, her eyes fixed on the raw scratches along his forearms, the blue-black bruises already beginning to show along his left shoulder.

'What happened to you?'

He wheeled about and the smile on his lips froze her where she stood, curtailing further questions. That strange smile again. Almost one of satisfaction—enjoyment. Someone had hurt him badly, yet he smiled as if it was of no importance. What could have happened to take precedence over the brutal beating he had received?

Hesitantly she advanced into the rooms, reached out tentatively to touch his bruised shoulder. He recoiled instantly. 'I'm sorry, did I hurt you? Let me help you.'

'No, dammit! What are you doing here?' he demanded in a fierce tone.

'I came to ask you to deliver a letter to Sancho. Felipe, in heaven's name, what has happened? You did not go to Pinos Altos?'

'Why ask such a stupid question?' he snapped, striding past her, angry-faced.

She stared after him in growing confusion, watching as he threw open the closet and selected a shirt and a blue silk cravat.

'You said—at the waterhole this morning.'

'Waterhole?' He rounded on her, his brown eyes narrowing. It was almost as if the morning no longer existed for him, Ysanne thought as she followed him into the bedroom, but he could not shut his mind to dead men and cattle! 'Oh, that.' Again, as if it was of no importance. Six good, trustworthy men lost and he did not care?

'Yes, that! Do you realise the grief among our people tonight? A father lost. A husband or son—a sweetheart! Our people are no longer happy, Felipe.' She had not meant to broach the subject until a more suitable time, but the words slipped out. The *peónes* who dwelt within the walls of the *hacienda* were as much her responsibility as his. She would not fail them and in doing so, fail the father who had cared and protected them for many years.

'I have already told them if they wish to leave they may do so.'

'Have you taken leave of your senses? Some of them were born on our land. Most have raised their children here. The graveyard is full of those who have died protecting anyone possessing the name of de Rivas. Whatever has made you so heartless?'

'Women without their men are of no use to me.' Felipe faced her, hands on his hips, his expression taut and guarded. Against her of all people! The thought further confused her. He was changing day by day, growing further away from her when they should have been growing closer. He spoke of the two of them fighting side by side, yet he chose to fight alone now, not asking her help or consulting her as to his methods. He had set loyal *peónes* against them, was intent on marrying her to a man he knew she did not love in return for support of arms and additional men. A thousand accusations came screaming into her throbbing brain and it took all the willpower she possessed to shut them out.

A livid bruise was beginning to show on one cheek and there was a deep scratch beneath one eye, reaching almost to the corner of his mouth. The mark of a wild animal, was her first instinctive thought, then for the second time in a few days her thoughts turned to that day in the high country when Ruy had been clawed by the cougar. She had seen the marks inflicted by the animal's claws and as she gingerly tried to stem the flow of blood from the wounds, he had remarked drily, 'Women are fickle creatures. I try to help her and she leaves her mark on me!'

The marks she had seen on Felipe were not deep

enough to be made by an animal and she felt herself gripped by a sudden chilling fear.

'Don't gape. What's the matter with you?' he demanded, drawing on his shirt. Long, deep scratches ran down the backs of the hands which fastened the buttons. 'After this morning I'm not surprised you can't stand the sight of blood.'

'You remember—?'

'Ysanne, what is wrong with you? I was there, wasn't I? I should not have taken you, I realise that now, but I was angry. Too angry. I thought you should see for yourself.'

'I did. You convinced me.' Then, she almost added, but that last word was never uttered as her brother turned from the mirror to stare into her pale features. '*Dios!* I have frightened you twice in one day. This morning it was intentional, but not now. This,' he touched his cheek and looked down at his hands with a shrug. 'It is nothing, just something I must bear alone.'

'As your sister do I not have the right to know? To help if I can?'

His lacerated face creased into a painful smile, so different from when he had been in the dressing-room and, as always, she became aware of the tremendous charm he could radiate at will, whatever the circumstances.

'Always these days, my sister, I am asking for your help. Do you not think it time I stood on my own two feet? Father may look down kindly on me then.'

'Why should he do otherwise, Felipe?'

'He was—loved—by everyone. I have no one.'

'You have me.' Was she wrong, or from the depths of her memory could she not recall other times like this? A wild bout of temper, cruelty, afterwards the necessity to talk, as if to rationalise that what he had done had been right, no matter what the outcome. A little boy kneeling by his bed, atoning for the sins of the day by saying he was sorry!

'What would I do without you? Was I curt just now?' He took her hands in his and she stiffened at his touch. Red hot, as if a fever were upon him, but there was no sign of perspiration on his skin. 'Don't look at me so strangely. I am fighting for our existence! Our lives! You are the last person from whom I expect condemnation.'

'Why should I condemn you? I came to give you a letter for Sancho and I find you bloody and bruised. I ask only that you tell me what has happened.'

'*Lo siento!* My mind reels. It was so full of remorse for what I did to you this morning, I did not realise I had ridden into a trap until it was too late.'

'A trap,' Ysanne echoed, her fingers tightened over his. 'Tell me.'

'For hours we followed useless tracks, backwards and forwards. Away from the waterhole, towards Pinos Altos, then towards the ranch, only to have them disappear in the dust.' As those that led away from the body of Pedro Valdez had vanished, Ysanne thought. Felipe, oh, my brother, say something to dispel the terrible suspicions I have about you. I know they cannot be possible!

For you I have cast aside the man I love, listened with scorn and disbelief to his brother Juan and treated Manuela as a foolish child, when I am little more myself. Help me! Tell me how wrong I am to have even one untrustworthy thought in my head about you. We are of the same blood. We cannot be so different. It is impossible!

'We found nothing,' Felipe continued, unaware of her agony of mind. 'But then Juan always was an excellent tracker, was he not? Or so you used to tell me after one of your exploits together. Impossible to follow, you once said. He was today.'

'If it was Juan, you could not have followed him in the beginning.'

'I know of no other with such skill in this part of the country. Doubtless that renegade Navajo, Chato, aided him. He is the only other one who could have obliterated signs of their treachery. Maybe they are working as a team, with Ruy as the schemer. Think on it, Ysanne. If he controlled the waterhole and the Valle de Lágrimas. Thousands of acres of land . . . with him owning the only access to water.'

'Papa owned and controlled it without trouble,' she reminded him, her lips beginning to tremble slightly.

'He never appreciated the great power he held in his hands. Some men need to, you know. It is like a drug to them. They have to feel it, savour it, like a good meal after a hard day's work. Something to be cossetted, cared for. Not always appreciated like a woman, but always the most predominant thing in their lives.'

'I don't understand you when you talk this way, Felipe.'

'Why? Because I appreciate what is mine? No one else will ever have it while I live.'

Mine! Not ours! Was this how he really intended it to be? If she married Sancho, the ranch would always be his, but the Valle de Lágrimas was still hers. He gained nothing except Sancho's friendship and support through the marriage and she was sure they already had that.

'What happened?' she asked again.

With a groan Felipe tore himself away and slumped into a chair, his face in his hands.

'I cannot tell you. I cannot!'

'You must,' she insisted, kneeling at his side. 'Felipe, do I not share your trust any longer? Who has hurt you so abominably?'

'Juan Valdez!'

'How?' Was her first question and then. 'When?'

'I was on my way back here after leaving the men at the waterhole, concealed this time. If Ruy dares to put any men or cattle near it, they will be as ours were this morning. No quarter, Ysanne. The choice was theirs.'

And you revel in the expectation of what might happen, she thought, as she looked at the wicked gleam in his eyes. You say otherwise, yet I feel in my heart you want war. Almost as if you enjoy the needless slaughter; need it, as others need power. As he had enjoyed freeing their father's horses when he was young and blatantly lied so that another took the blame—and the punishment. Before she went away, he had taken no part in the running of the ranch. Now he was its master and she was finding herself unwanted. Unneeded.

'Go on.' As she spoke she heard the ominous rumble of thunder in the distance. The storm was approaching.

'No quarter to any of them. Do you hear me? Only her—she must be saved before they contaminate her. I tried to tell her, but she . . . no, he, would not let her listen. She has learned now he is no match for Felipe de Rivas. It may give her the courage she needs to come to me.'

'What have you done?' Ysanne asked, aghast, and he looked up at her with wide, innocent eyes.

'Done? I defended her against him. She is mine!'

'Do you mean Manuela?'

'Of course. We met as I rode home. Oh, Ysanne, she was so pleased to see me. If only you could have heard the things she said, felt the touch of her lips against mine disproving all their foolish lies.'

Ysanne stepped back from him. It was as if the thunder was suddenly in the room with them, deafening her. She felt the hardness of a chair against her legs, but dared not sit down. Felipe was no longer looking at her, but past her. He was seeing nothing but the images in his own mind, she realised. Stepping past the chair, she stood with her weight against the huge bureau by the window. Her hands clenched into tight fists behind her back; the knuckles white. Manuela had ridden home with Juan. There was no doubt in her mind—he would not have left her for an instant. Their love was something she could no longer deny. Why was Felipe still lying about their relationship? Or was it something he just did not accept and was therefore not real to him?

'My poor Ysanne. I speak of tenderness and love and you think of Ruy, do you not?' Felipe said softly and she felt herself blush. 'Have I not proved he is not for you? With Sancho you will be content, believe me.'

'Content!' Ysanne cried. 'I want love, not contentment. You seek it, demand it from Manuela, yet it is denied me. Are we so different?'

'But of course.' Rising to his feet, Felipe turned

back to the dresser and began to slip onyx links into the cuffs of his shirt. 'I repeat, Ruy will not have you. Accept it. Manuela, on the other hand, is the perfection I seek; require. We are a kindred spirit. Once joined we will never be parted. My dear, I care for you very much and I want to see you settled with the right man. Sancho is older, but not without fire. You should see him with some of the women in town. No, perhaps not. His affection for you is genuine. I do know that.'

If only I could believe yours was for me, Ysanne thought miserably. You do not even understand the love I speak of. I do not need Ruy. I desire him. Once I wished to spend the rest of my life with him. Not need—love! You have never known it or you could not be so eager to send me to the bed of another man. I am a useful commodity to be bartered to the highest bidder. Sancho has powerful friends in high places and many men and you have taken advantage of his loneliness in order to gain these things in the future. The sickness within her swelled. Pulling on a dark *charro* jacket, Felipe smoothed the silk ruffles down over his hands, stared at his reflection and smiled.

'Those marks, Felipe, how did you get them?' she heard herself asking, as if from a great distance.

'I told you, I was attacked by Juan Valdez.'

'Juan? but that is not possible . . .'

'Were you there? Did you see the way he launched himself at me like a madman? He saw us together, Manuela in my arms, where she was always meant to be. I made her ride away quickly before he did her harm. He thought he could best me—the fool!'

The last two words were spoken so quietly Ysanne hardly heard them. A vivid zig-zag of lightning burst through the windows into the room and with an annoyed oath, Felipe pulled the curtains and lighted another lamp. Fresh shadows slanted across his face, concealing his expression from her. For some reason she was glad.

'You fought with Juan?' She forced the words through stiff lips. She had never expected to experience again the kind of bone-chilling fear she had felt at her father's death, but it was with her again. This time, it was a nightmare of a different kind. She knew he was lying and what little hope and trust she had placed in their relationship after that terrible ordeal, began to crumble in the face of these new lies.

The questions she had ignored or refused to answer, steadfast in her trust of her brother, now crowded into her mind, demanding satisfaction.

'Have I not told you twice? Are you not listening to me? He found me with Manuela and attacked me. Once she was safely out of the way, I retaliated and would have beaten him, but when he saw he was losing, he had two *vaqueros* intervene and drag me off him. Then he watched while they beat me, damn him. He did not want me killed, he said, only taught a lesson. Give me your letter and let me go.' Felipe held out his hand and like some mechanical doll she reached into her pocket and gave it to him. So calm now, so casual. Apart from the scratch on his face no one would know the traumatic experience he had been through.

You must believe him, he is your brother, her heart demanded. Perhaps Juan and Manuela had been joined by two men from the ranch as they rode homewards, but even so, that would not explain his description of the reception he received. 'Pleased to see me . . . the things she said . . . the touch of her lips.' The words hammered at her brain. Only a few hours ago Manuela had vehemently denied an association with Felipe, spoken of her fear of him, her love for Juan Valdez!

What had Felipe to gain from these lies? And then on the heels of this question, impossible for her to answer, came others, more sinister in their implications. Far more frightening. Did those marks on his face betray what really happened when he met Manuela? Had she fought him, raking his cheeks with her nails, the hands that sought to detain, perhaps caress her, in an effort to escape?

'Am I to expect an answer to this?' her brother asked as he thrust the letter into an inside pocket.

'*Sí*. I have invited Sancho to dine with us on Saturday. You don't mind, do you?'

'On the contrary, it will give us a chance to have a long talk. Do you intend to put the poor man out of his misery at long last?'

'I intend to do just that,' Ysanne replied.

'I can see by your face you are still angry with me for this morning.' He slipped a finger beneath her chin and tilted back her head. His tone was quite light and untroubled. The beating he had received seemed forgotten. 'You must allow me to manage things my way from now on, my sister. I tried to be lenient for your sake, but as you have seen, it has not worked. Now I fight by Ruy's mehods. An eye for an eye. I will strike at everything, everyone who is important to him. He will soon learn, as his brother did, that Felipe de Rivas has a sting too. A deadly one. You say nothing! So you have resigned yourself to your loss at last. Sancho will be pleased to hear it.'

'Let me tell him,' Ysanne pleaded.

'Certainly. We will make it a day to remember.'

It will be, Ysanne thought as they parted, especially when you learn I have been to Pinos Altos.

'Bring me something to eat on a tray,' she ordered Serafina an hour later. Most of that time she had been standing by the bedroom window, watching the approach of dark rain clouds, which now totally filled the sky. The thunder was growing closer. She did not like to listen to it even now, but she knew it would be useless to go to bed early. She would not sleep tonight and the storm was not to blame.

'What is troubling you, *mi niña*?' Serafina asked, staring down at the food she left untouched.

'Doubts,' Ysanne answered quietly. 'Doubts I know I should not have about my own brother. But I cannot help myself. Did you see him when he came home?'

'No, but Fernando said he looked as if he had been in a fight—and got the worst of it.'

'He told me he had been attacked by men from Pinos Altos, on the orders of Juan Valdez, but Juan and Manuela were alone when I left them. He had scratches on his hands and face, Serafina, he did not get those in a fight. They looked like,' Ysanne faltered, her lips trembling, 'like the kind of marks a woman's nails would make.'

Serafina gave a horrified gasp and crossed herself.

'I have been so wrapped up in myself these past weeks, I have not realised how much he is changing. I hardly know him. One moment we are close, the next he is a stranger, exactly as it was when we were children.'

'Don Diego once said the same thing to me. They were always quarrelling those first few months after you went away, I remember, and always over trivialities. Only after Don Diego's first seizure did your brother seem to take an interest in the ranch.'

'Don't go on. I wish I had never gone away. What good did it do? I achieved nothing. I have lost my father, my brother . . .' Ysanne curbed the desire to unburden her soul. Serafina would listen as she always did, give wise counsel, but biased, she suspected, in favour of the mistress she idolised. She did not want that. It was necessary for Ysanne herself to assess rationally and, most of all unemotionally, what was happening about her. After she had spoken to Ruy she would be able to evaluate events of the past few months.

'I still have not decided what to wear on Saturday, have I?' Ysanne began doubtfully. 'I suppose the green would do.'

'I found another while you were gone. Why you had pushed it behind all the others is a mystery. It is the most beautiful thing I have ever seen.'

The colour receded from Ysanne's cheeks at the dress produced. It was indeed the most exquisite gown she had ever possessed, the pride of her wardrobe—unworn. The elaborately tiered skirt was made up of a dozen layers of snow-white Cordoba lace, as was the low-cut bodice and the full, ruffled sleeves. Sewn into the intricate pattern of delicate rosebuds which covered the material were miniature white satin bows. It had been made for one purpose only, her homecoming ball, when she would have presented herself before Ruy Valdez, wearing her grandmother's diamonds and lace *mantilla*, beautifully gowned and confident of gaining and retaining his interest.

'It is almost like a wedding gown. This would melt the stoniest of hearts,' Serafina breathed in awe.

'No it will not and I was stupid to think otherwise. Put it away. No—wait!' Ysanne could not resist the temptation to hold it against her once again. It would be the last time. She would never wear it. There could never be an occasion important enough.

'All hearts but one, Serafina,' she said softly, touching the lace to her cheeks. 'It was for him. No one will ever see it now.'

'Put it on for me, just this once,' Serafina asked, greatly reluctant to hide away such a magnificent creation.

'Don't be silly!' And yet why not, if it helped to exorcise the ghost which haunted her? 'Very well. Then put it back and I never want to see it again.'

She had lost weight, Ysanne realised, the moment Serafina carefully lowered the dress over her head and began to hook up the fastenings. It clung more snugly to her hips and the neckline slipped a little more provocatively from slender tanned shoulders. Tía Dolores had almost thrown a fit, she remembered, when she saw it. Over exposed, had been her tight-lipped description; it could not possibly be worn while Ysanne was beneath her roof. Ysanne had smiled and assured her it never would be, looking forward, even more, to Ruy's initial reaction.

A sad smile touched her lips now as she gazed at her reflection. This was no time to dwell on what might have been or she could possibly weaken in her resolve to face Ruy and demand an explanation for his—to her at least—unexplainable and unforgivable actions. Tomorrow was going to be a very difficult and unpleasant day, she decided.

'Help me take it off now, Serafina. Do you hear me?'

The woman stood transfixed as if with shock and her mouth was beginning to gape. Ysanne spun round towards the french windows. The scream which rose in her throat at the sight of the face outside died unuttered on her lips as Ruy Valdez stepped quickly into the room, with Chato the Indian close on his heels, and the guns in their hands froze her into silence.

CHAPTER SEVEN

Was it the blast of cold air from outside which accompanied their arrival, or the sight of the murderous expression in Ruy's eyes, which chilled her to the bone? His gaze raked her from head to toe and she watched a sardonic twist deepen the lean mouth as he considered the elegant gown she wore. It had been meant for him, but this was not how he should have first seen it!

'I see Felipe has wasted no time in persuading you to the advantages of marriage to a man of Sancho's importance.'

She blanched at the insult. He thought it looked like a wedding gown too!

'Are you mad to come here?' At last she found her voice. How had they passed unnoticed under the nose of the guard on the gate? 'You will be killed. My brother has ordered no quarter after this morning.'

'We were not seen.' He accurately read her immediate thought. 'We left our horses beyond the walls and followed in the wake of some mourners returning home. No one noticed a few extra men in the dark. So Felipe gives no quarter. He shall have some of his own medicine.'

'What are you doing here? What do you want?' Ysanne demanded, slowly beginning to recover some of her composure. As her self-control returned, her gaze centred contemptuously on the weapon aimed at her body. Ruy replaced it in the holster about his waist. Chato made no move to follow suit. As suspicious of her as always, she thought.

'Justice, and this time I intend to deal it out personally. Where is Felipe?' came the stony reply.

'Out—at a cattlemen's meeting. What do you want with him?' There were very few servants in the house who could come to her aid, she realised. Most people had gone to the funerals of the murdered men. The full force of the men would still be at the cemetery a full mile away.

'I am going to kill him.'

She gave an involuntary gasp and stepped back, a hand against her mouth.

'Chato, check his room. The second door on your left out of here,' Ruy ordered. 'Be careful, *amigo*. She could be lying.'

The man made no sound as he crossed the room on moccasined feet, opened the door and vanished into the corridor. She had forgotten how silently he moved. Like a shadow.

She tried a dozen times to speak, but the words stuck in her throat. Thank God Felipe had gone out. Chato returned as silently as he went, the swarthy face registering annoyance as he shook his head.

'I told you he was out, now will you go?'

'Not yet. He was only part of the reason I risked coming here. I came for you too,' Ruy said in a flat tone. 'Will you come willingly or must I resort to force. Make no mistake, I will if I have to.'

'Force,' Ysanne echoed, then, as the full implication of his words sank into her, she grew deathly pale. 'You mean to abduct me? You are mad! Why? Did Juan not tell you I was coming to Pinos Altos tomorrow to talk to you?'

'My brother lies unconscious back at the *hacienda* and Manuela is half out of her mind with what she witnessed this afternoon. The attempted murder of the man she loves—by your brother.'

Where? How? she wanted to ask, but the expression on his face deterred her. He believed Felipe to have deliberately attacked Juan and had come seeking revenge.

Recollection of that bloodstained shirt on the chair in her brother's room rose in her mind, the sight of him standing before her, bruised, bloodied. It could not be, yet in her heart she knew that Ruy was speaking the truth. The scratches Felipe had received had been made in desperation, even panic. He was her brother, but she could no longer dismiss the terrible doubts crowding in on her. She could not allow Ruy to take her . . . One last chance she would give him, that of escape, if she could find him in time and warn him.

She wheeled towards the door, but cannoned into Serafina standing directly behind her. Before she could go on, she was seized from behind. A kerchief was bound around her mouth, roughly gagging her, the arm around her waist effectively pinioning her arms to her sides.

'Something to tie her with, quickly,' Ruy snapped and his companion snatched one of the cords from the curtains and flung it to him, before crossing the space separating him from Serafina and pushing her bodily down on to the bed. As he was about to bind her too, Ruy intervened, 'No, leave her free. She is going to escort us safely to the gate.'

Although she was strong and agile and struggled continuously, Ysanne was no match against the man who held her and, within minutes, her wrists had been securely bound behind her. In the struggle her hair had fallen free of confining combs to tumble like tongues of fire about her shoulders and her face was flushed with angry colour.

Even in the midst of the grief and fury which engulfed him, the overwhelming desire for revenge, the man who stepped back from her still thought she was the loveliest creature he had ever seen.

'Get up, woman,' he ordered curtly. 'Give me a cloak to cover your mistress.'

Ysanne made muffled sounds of protest behind the gag and shook her head frantically, but Serafina obeyed. She was enveloped from head to toe in a dark blue cloak, the hood pulled well over her face. In the darkness they might very well succeed in their attempt to kidnap her!

'Be still,' Ruy snapped as he took her arm and she began to struggle again. 'I give you fair warning, Ysanne, if you do not behave yourself, I will knock you out cold and carry you out. And kill anyone who gets in my way. Isn't that what you would expect of me anyway? You have tried and condemned me in your heart. I only hope you will be able to live with yourself when you know the truth.'

She glared at him, her lovely eyes expressing all the things she could not put into words at that moment. He was not gentle as he propelled her out on to the verandah and down the side staircase, Chato and Serafina following close behind.

There were fires burning in the square, but few

people about. Tonight they were behind closed doors, mourning the loss of loved ones. She saw the gates were still open, confirming the fact that most of the villagers had not yet returned. Ruy had chosen his time well. Only one sentry guarded the gateway to freedom.

He stopped and pulled her into the shadows. As she resisted he pushed her against the wall, holding her still with the weight of his body. Looking at Serafina he said in a low tone,

'If he sees us there will be more blood spilt, perhaps that of your mistress. Will you risk that?'

'I will do nothing to harm a hair on her head,' the woman retorted in a fierce whisper, 'but if you lay one finger on her . . .'

'A veritable she-wolf,' Chato growled out of the darkness. 'Let me take the sentry.'

'No. There has been enough needless killing, besides, an unguarded gate would immediately arouse suspicion. Talk to him, woman, while we slip through and you have my word your mistress will not be harmed. Believe it or not I am about to save her from her own foolishness, though she'll not thank me for it when she knows what is ahead for her.'

'Don Diego said you would always come to her aid if she needed it.'

Ruy muttered an expletive under his breath. 'I always knew you listened at keyholes. You know too much, I don't like that.'

'My lips are sealed, for her sake.' Serafina lightly touched Ysanne's cheeks, instantly drawing back with a hurt expression on her face as she flinched away. 'I must do what he says. Believe me, it is better you go with him.'

Ysanne could not believe her ears. Betrayed by Serafina, the only friend she had ever totally trusted since childhood! With a soft moan she sagged in Ruy's grasp, her senses reeling, aware of him forcing her towards the gate as Serafina drew the guard into conversation and his back was towards them. When her steps faltered, he swept her up into his arms and ran the last few yards to where the horses were tethered.

After an hour of hard travelling they were starting upwards towards the high country. By that time Ysanne ached in every limb from the fast pace they had maintained since leaving the house. She had sat bolt upright, seated across his saddle, determined not to relax against him no matter how uncomfortable the ride became. But the severe jolting she was receiving she was sure threatened to break her back and when Ruy's arm tightened around her waist, drawing her back against him, she was wise enough to offer no resistance. Deliberately she kept her face averted, staring straight ahead of her so that he would not take her acceptance of his action as a sign of weakness, or surrender, and yet at the same moment as that thought was in her head, there was another. To allow her aching limbs to settle against the firmness of his body, her head to fall back against a broad shoulder. And so much more she knew she would never dare put into words to anyone!

Dark clouds now obscured the moon as the storm followed close in their wake. As the first trees began to close in all around them and the heavy scent of pine and firs invaded her nostrils, Ruy pulled the hood from her head and eased the gag from her mouth. They were in his territory now and she sensed he felt safe. Chato, following some distance behind them, was ensuring they were not being followed.

'My wrists hurt,' she complained, when he made no move to loosen her bonds. How could he be so indifferent to her discomfort?

'Perhaps a little pain will bring you to your senses,' came the callous retort and instantly she bristled.

'Have you not given me enough of that already,' she said fiercely.

Her loose hair was wound around his fist and tugged painfully back until her face was but a few inches from his and she was able to see the fury glittering in those dark pools.

'Do not try my patience, Ysanne. I have little left for you, or anyone else.'

'By morning you will have every one of my brother's *vaqueros* on your doorstep,' she flung back bravely. 'With Felipe leading them.'

'*Bueno*.' He gave a nod of satisfaction. 'I would like that.'

'It is what you want? And you speak of no more senseless killings?' she breathed, her eyes dilating in horror. 'Felipe is right. You do want open warfare between us.'

'I want only your brother, not the Hacienda de las Flores, or the Valle de Lágrimas. Nothing but him. He has to be stopped and I am the only one who can do it. I have to, before the ground flows red with more blood spilt to achieve his ambitions. He has stained it three times already with that of innocent people who were close to us. I am determined it will not happen again.'

'What is it I do not know?' she cried in great

agitation and his expression grew even more pitiless. The fear mirrored in her eyes touched him, but he knew this was no time for weakness. Time and time again, since he had whisked her from the house, he had cursed the dying man who had extracted a promise from him which brought him neither pleasure nor satisfaction, as once it might have done. He was a fool to have kept it, no one would know had he not. Ysanne's contempt—no, hatred, for that was what she surely felt for him—would multiply once they reached Pinos Altos and she learned what awaited her.

'It is too late to ask questions. You should have done that when you came home.'

'I did! No one had answers for me, least of all you! And then Papa died . . .'

'You did not say "was killed",' he intervened harshly. 'Are you beginning to doubt Felipe's story? Be careful. One crack in your safe little world might grow into a chasm. When you fall into it, *chica*, there is going to be nothing to grab hold of and you are going all the way to the bottom. It is going to hurt like hell.'

'You should enjoy the spectacle.'

'Why? As some kind of twisted satisfaction gained for that scene you played at Diego's funeral? Few people swallowed that story, least of all me. You were annoyed because your father had brought you home, depriving you of the company of all those *guapos hombres* in Monterey. Your aunt implied quite firmly that you had chosen a husband. She may have approved of your choice, but your father certainly did not, which is why he decided to bring you home. You would have accepted the marriage in time, he was certain of that. I did not share his optimism.'

Ysanne was silent for a long while, then the horse, stumbling on uneven ground, jerked her back to reality.

'Marriage?' Her father had arranged everything and not told her. The letter she had never received had obviously been telling her of his plans, but she had never received it because she had decided to come home. Had his deteriorating health prompted him to act so swiftly and alone?

'Come now, why so alarmed? Am I not the man you chose yourself of your own free will? The man for whom you went to Monterey to that dragon of an aunt to learn how to be a good wife?' His sardonic tone brought a rush of tears to her eyes. She could not hide them from him for he was still holding fast to her hair. 'It is too late for those too. They will not move me from my chosen path. Whether you like it or not I am going to save you from making a terrible mistake. I gave Diego my word . . .' he broke off, as if regretting he might have been too open with her, released her hair and concentrated on the trail ahead.

Ysanne was too shattered by his revelation to utter another word. That very day she had returned he had been on his way to see her father, to complete the marriage contract. Her dreams would have come true in a few short hours but for the vicious attack which had brought about her father's death. Why had he quarrelled with Ruy? If the valley was what Ruy wanted, then marriage to her would have given it to him upon her death, should there be no surviving female. Anyway, as her husband, Ysanne would have had no objections to him taking it over and caring for it. Then she had trusted him . . . Still, he had no reason to kill for it!

The tears flowed faster as her confusion grew. By the time they reached Pinos Altos, she was too exhausted even to demand answers to her questions.

Ruy lifted her from the saddle, supporting her against him until she eased her cramped limbs and then immediately moved away from him.

Pinos Altos was aptly named. The tall pines surrounding it towered to the sky. Many had been cleared when the house was built. It was not surrounded by a high wall as was her own home, but stood in a clearing, stark compared to the approach to the Hacienda de las Flores, with neither trees nor flower beds. Yet somehow it suited the place and the men who dwelt within it. The *vaqueros* and their families had chosen to make their homes on land in the nearby vicinity. A different kind of freedom, Ysanne realised, as she stared around her.

The house dominated the scene, some three or four hundred yards in front of her. To her left were stables and houses, storage barns and a huge corral. To her right, the village proper, with many buildings, vegetable gardens and orchards blooming with more intensity than she had ever seen in the past. The crop would be good this year, sustaining everyone. Ruy had always possessed a self-sufficient streak. The people in his care had always been his prime concern. Yet predominant over this memory of him, was the recollection of him striding from her father's study, his face like thunder. Angry, dangerous, deadly! If she was wrong in her condemnation, why did he not exonerate himself with a satisfactory explanation? He did not have one was the only answer which ever came back to her to sink her deeper into the depths of despair. He could not explain and Felipe had lied. She could trust no one!

The sound of singing began to penetrate her stunned mind. Women's voices—not singing—it was almost a lament.

'What—what is happening?' she demanded and tried, without succeeding, to sound in control of herself.

'The Navajo women mourn their dead. The men your brother killed yesterday,' came the cold reply. Not from Ruy, but Chato. She had no answer, yet again. 'Men from your *rancho* were murdered, so too were men from here—and women also who went to cook for them, and a young boy . . . my son. Murdered by your brother! Only the wise words of my *amigo*, *el patrón*, stopped me sending the other men here on a death mission. He said it will end soon. He will end this bloodshed. He is my friend and I believe him, but I am still a Navajo. When the blood of my people flows, I cry vengeance, and vengeance I will have, no matter how long it takes. Your brother is a dead man, señorita!'

The door was flung open and bright lamplight flooded into the area before the house. Ruy's arm encircled her shoulders as a figure materialised from the shadows and a friendly voice, which she recognised belonged to the local priest, Father Simón, declared,

'Ruy, at last! I have been here hours, my son. Where have you been?'

'Forgive me, Padre, there was something I had to

do. You have seen Juan? How is he? Is he conscious yet?'

'Slowly, my boy. Slowly. He has not yet opened his eyes, but his breathing has improved and I shall stay with him and pray at his side until he recovers consciousness, with God's merciful help. You must make Manuela rest. The poor child looks quite exhausted and when I asked her how Juan came to be injured, she acted most strangely.'

'I will answer all your questions when I have seen her to bed and looked in on my brother,' Ruy assured him.

'Doña Ysanne! What are you doing here?' For the first time the priest recognised the pale-faced girl at the side of Ruy Valdez.

'I have brought you here on an errand of mercy, also on one of rejoicing in our moment of crisis.' The fingers on Ysanne's shoulders dug suddenly, painfully deep. 'I have told you of Don Diego's last wishes. Ysanne has come here tonight to fulfill them. Have you not, my love?'

She opened her mouth to deny the words and his lips were on hers without warning, silencing her until she had no breath to speak. Ruy broke from her with a soft chuckle.

'Father, forgive us. In the midst of sadness we are about to find happiness. Will you be ready for us in an hour? Come, my love!'

Again that insulting term. She saw by the smile on Father Simón's face that he accepted every word spoken. Bound wrists, encumbered by the cloak about her, propelled by the strong arm about her shoulders, Ysanne could do nothing but obey.

My love! He would pay for those careless endearments, she vowed, as she was hurried upstairs and thrust, without consideration once they were beyond the vision of the priest, into a side room.

The terrifyingly sharp knife Ruy took from his belt sliced through her bonds without effort. Coldly he regarded her as she chafed bloodless wrists.

'An hour, that is all you have, Ysanne. Either you marry me as your father wished—here, tonight—or you come to my bed without a ring. The choice is yours. It matters not to me.'

The door slammed behind him and she was alone. An hour to decide the rest of her life. A choice! She had not and yet . . .

It matters not to me . . . He would have her—his wife or not! She sank down on to the edge of the bed, shivering. Cold, fear, she did not know which gave her more discomfort. If only he had said she *must* wed him. To take her without a ring meant he cared nothing for her, despite all his fancy promises to her father. If they had been made. He intended to keep her at Pinos Altos and use her . . . For a moment she had almost believed him!

When he returned she was standing by the window. The storm had reached Pinos Altos and the sky was as bright as day as vivid lightning criss-crossed the sky and the countryside echoed with the sound of thunder. Like an angry mountain about to erupt, she thought as she turned to face him.

'You are ready . . .' he began, then the words died on his lips.

She had brushed her hair and rearranged it so that not a single strand was out of place. She was still pale, but composed. He inwardly marvelled at her self-control, but was unable to tell her how much he admired it and respected her. Too much had passed between them. Too many bitter words, accusations—lies!

Disdainfully Ysanne picked up the skirts of her exquisite gown, moved past him into the corridor and the emeralds in her eyes were the coldest he had ever seen. It was like looking into a mirror and he did not like it at all!

'I will do as you wish. I have no choice, but if you ever attempt to—to take me against my will, I will kill you—and the Valle de Lágrimas can go to the devil!' she challenged defiantly.

'We are in agreement at last,' came the dry retort.

'You—you really do not want it?' she faltered.

'No.' Such fierceness in his tone. It had to be the truth. 'How much more blood must be spilled before you believe me?'

He turned and stared at her as they reached the head of the stairs.

'I will never take you by force, you should know that. How will you be taken, Ysanne? Or, is it possible, you can give some part of yourself still?'

'In love.' The words fell from lips that trembled visibly and he frowned.

'That is beyond both of us now. Come.'

He took her arm and led her downstairs. As her steps faltered and she tried to draw back from him, she found herself face to face with Father Simón.

'I have told the good father this is a love match, with your father's blessing,' he whispered in her ear as they approached. 'You will not contest that. Our marriage will stop the bloodshed once and for all.'

'You say that when less than an hour ago you told me you intend to kill Felipe. What kind of peace is that?'

'If Juan dies, your brother will die by my hand. Perhaps he will realise, in time, that he has nothing to gain once he has lost the Valle de Lágrimas.'

'Ysanne, my child, it is a brave thing you do in the midst of all this trouble and grief. I hope it will go some way to reuniting Ruy and Felipe again.'

'I doubt that, Father. Too much has happened,' Ruy answered before she could find her tongue. 'But we all hope for a miracle, don't we?'

'I will pray you are wrong, my son. This madness which has descended over you all must surely end soon.'

'Madness indeed,' Ruy echoed and there was an oddness in his tone which made her look at him sharply, but his expression told her nothing.

He had changed into a fresh white shirt that accentuated the darkness of his skin and she had to steel herself not to respond to his touch as he took her fingers and touched them to his lips.

'Let me go,' she whispered, in a tone which did not go beyond them. 'If you do not want the valley, prove it! Let me leave here now.'

His eyes considered her for a long moment with an intensity that was disturbing.

'Will that prove to you I am innocent of all the charges Felipe has laid against me—of your own nasty suspicions? If you leave here you will do so in the knowledge you have refused to carry out your father's dying wishes. You bear him a strange love, Ysanne, if you do that.'

'That is not fair,' she protested. He had struck at her most vulnerable spot.

'Have you been with me? No. You will stay and you will say nothing to upset the good father. He believes this to be your wish too.'

Chato and his Navajo mother, a woman very much like Serafina in size, with jet-black hair despite her sixty years, came into the room and he moved away from her to speak to them.

'My dear child, you do not know how happy I am to have carried out your father's dearest wish.'

The three of them stood before a blazing fire in the *sala*, yet despite the warmth coming from the flames leaping in the huge wrought-iron basket which dominated the chasm of a fireplace, Ysanne was acutely conscious of how cold she was. Not even the potency of the full-bodied sherry she was drinking seemed to penetrate the coldness of her limbs or dispel the numbness which had closed over her mind as Ruy slipped a thick gold band on to her finger.

She was his wife now! His property! What if he had lied? No, she had to face the facts, unpleasant as they were, Felipe was the liar. About his relationship with Manuela, which she herself knew to be false, and so many other things she had never thought, or dared to question him about because he was her brother and she loved and trusted him. She loved Ruy too, but because of the seeds of suspicion and mistrust Felipe had sown in her mind, she had grown almost afraid of him, of what he might have become while she was away.

If accepting that her brother had fabricated a tissue of lies for his own purposes, and what they were was still beyond her, she knew she must now cast aside his statement that Ruy had struck the blow which injured her father. Until this moment she had accepted it. Now it was in dispute, but the alternative . . . Could Felipe have killed his own father? For what reason? He had always had everything he wanted. She drew in her breath so sharply that Ruy cast a questioning look in her direction. She pretended not to notice. She had suddenly realised that Felipe did not have everything he wanted. He did not have the one thing he craved more than anything else in the world—the person he adored, worshipped, wove fantasies about because she was out of his reach. Manuela!

The implications which followed in the wake of this awesome realisation were terrible to contemplate, but she knew she had to go through them calmly, rationally.

'Are you all right, Ysanne?' Ruy was still staring at her and she nodded wordlessly, turning away to seat herself in a chair. He followed her, his eyes dark with thought as he bent to refill her glass, despite her protest she had had enough. 'Drink up, Father Simón has eyes like a hawk,' he murmured. 'In a little while you and I will settle what is between us.'

'You have given me little reason to celebrate. Dragging me here like a sack of potatoes, forcing me to marry you. Don't worry, I won't betray your farce by breaking down in tears before him. I have none left.' I shed them all for you, she thought as he moved away with an annoyed frown at her rebuff.

It took a while to force her thoughts back to the conclusion she had just reached before he spoke to her. Manuela was the key to everything, not the Valle de Lágrimas. He wanted only her! Pedro Valdez had been against the marriage and he was dead! Her father, who had also opposed it once he knew of the girl's feelings for Juan, was also in his grave! Juan, who stood between Felipe and the woman he desired, lay unconscious upstairs! Ruy, the man who now controlled Manuela's future, had been accused of being a liar and a thief—a murderer! Anyone capable of posing the slightest problems was either dead or under suspicion of some heinous crime. Was Felipe capable of so coldbloodedly disposing of all opposition? What kind of mind could devise such diabolical schemes?

'Ruy!' A girl's shrill tones sounded outside the room and he immediately wheeled towards the door with Father Simón on his heels. Wine splashed on the skirts of Ysanne's gown as she pushed her glass on to a table and hurried after them.

Manuela stood swaying at the top of the massive pine staircase, her eyes wide with distress.

'Where is the doctor, Ruy? Why does he not come?' she cried as he reached her side and took her in his arms. She was totally unaware of the other two figures behind him. 'Juan will die, I know it.'

'Hush, child, he will not die! You are tired. Come to bed. Father Simón will sit with Juan. No arguments. When you see him in the morning he will be better.'

She did not resist as he led her to a room further along the corridor. Ysanne forced herself to look into Juan's room as she passed. It was dark with shadows and the oil lamp beside the bed was turned down very low. There was no sound of breathing, no movement, and she shivered as if chilled by a cold wind. The priest moved past her, patted her gently, reassuringly, on the shoulder and went inside, closing the door behind him.

'Is there anything I can do?' she asked as Ruy

returned. His expression was once more distant, his thoughts elsewhere.

'Go to bed,' he said curtly and a bitter smile touched her lips.

'Aren't you afraid I might run away without someone watching me?'

'Where will you run to? You are my wife now, out of reach of Sancho, therefore of no further use to Felipe who hoped for arms and men from his brother-in-law.'

She grew pale at the insinuation, knowing he was right. She must accept the fact she had been used as she must accept everything else that had happened. She brushed past him, her eyes full of bright tears.

He came into the room some ten minutes later and tossed some night-clothes onto the bed.

'Manuela sent these for you.' His tone was impersonal, not so the light which suddenly flickered in his eyes as he looked across the room to where she stood.

'Thank her for me.'

Ysanne did not move from the window. What now? Had he come expecting his rights as her husband? She flinched as a violent boom of thunder shook the room and the glass chandelier swayed with the immense vibration. Moments later came the lightning, illuminating the room again and again in an eerie silence. Ruy moved towards her. Halted close enough to touch her, but did not.

'God willing, one day you will understand why this was necessary. It is the only way I can protect you.'

'You keep saying that. Protect me from what? Who? You owe me an explanation.'

'I owe you nothing. I have kept my promise to Diego and, as far as I am concerned, that is an end to it. Besides I never was one for explanations or excuses.'

'No, you were always your own man,' Ysanne said, in a tone which did not imply approval. 'You always went your own way, kept your own counsel and heaven help anyone foolish enough to—to care for you.'

'How lucky you are never to have been in that situation,' Ruy remarked humourlessly.

'Why did my father take you into his confidence?'

'You were not around, were you, *chica*? He needed someone he could trust.'

It should have been her, not him!

'Always you seek explanations,' Ruy scathed. 'Can you not trust for once in your life, or is it a way of easing your conscience because you were away when he needed you? To dream the dreams of a young girl is permissible, Ysanne, but upon your return, discovering how you had failed him, to use me as an excuse for your absence—that is unforgivable.'

'Would you permit yourself to be used, Ruy?' Ysanne asked boldly and the way she looked at him was a mixture of contempt and mockery, coupled with the nearest thing to a challenge he had ever seen. 'I went to Monterey for only one reason.' Ysanne spoke very slowly, very quietly, pausing as thunder again echoed overhead so that he would be able to hear every word she said. 'I wanted to grow up. To return a woman in your eyes, not the tomboy who rode and hunted at your side, shared your campfire, but not your heart and watched you dance with all my friends, but not me, because to you I was not a woman.'

'You go too far . . .' Ruy began, but she ignored both the interruption and his warning look.

'What do you know about love, Ruy? I will tell you—nothing! What would you give up for it? I gave up the things I cherished most in the hope of one day pleasing you—my home and the love of my father. I have lost both and gained nothing. *Sí*, you have kept a promise you made to him, but do not expect me to thank you for it. There is too much blood between us for us ever to share anything again.'

'That of your father?' he ejaculated angrily. 'You still believe . . .'

'No. But . . .'

'If you loved me there would be trust between us. Until we have that there can never be anything else. Love! *Dios*, you are the one who does not know what it means,' he flung back, tight-lipped.

'Why, because I will not blindly accept your word. I did once with Felipe . . .'

'So at last you have realised he has been using you, lying to you?' Ruy knew he should have felt great satisfaction at the revelation, in the knowledge she was no longer blinded by devotion to a brother bent on destroying her if she failed him, but instead he felt empty—drained.

'*Sí*. He—he . . .' She could not find the words. She was betraying Felipe! Her own flesh and blood! 'Sometimes it is as if he lives in another world. It was that way often when we were children. He used to frighten me, yet we could be so close.'

'At last you begin to understand.'

'What? You tell me nothing.'

'I tell you, you are safe here with me. Be content with that for the moment. If you ever see Felipe alone again, I am sure he will try to kill you. He has to now, you stand in his way.'

'He is my brother, not—not some deranged animal . . .' That smile! That odd smile that made her shiver each time she saw it. That faraway look in his eyes on occasions and the sudden, uncontrollable rages! Madness? No, it could not be? She was quite sane.

'Only a madman could callously strike down his own father and force his attentions on a young girl who detests him. Attempt to kill the man she loves.' They could have been her words! They were her thoughts! '*Lo siento!* I am sorry you will not believe me. At the moment I am more concerned with Juan's recovery than what you think of me. If he is better tomorrow, perhaps we will talk again.'

'And if he is not?' Ysanne ventured to ask, knowing the answer already.

'Then Felipe's blood will be on my hands. Don't be afraid to sleep, I won't disturb you. The choice was yours.' He turned away, then spun around and was at her side before she could move. His hands fastened over her shoulders, holding her powerless. 'Taken in love, you said. Show me some of this love you have for me, Ysanne! Let me taste it in your lips. Feel it in your body.'

She twisted her head away, but he was too strong for her. One arm encircled her waist, the other held the back of her head immobile as his mouth descended on hers, smothering her frightened cry. The passion in his kisses shocked her. She had no reserves of strength after what had taken place tonight to fight against this unexpected onslaught and her lips parted beneath his. He was kissing her as if he hated her, she realised, but there was nothing she could do about it. She moaned in his tight embrace, but he did not release her. Her senses began to reel as she felt herself lifted and carried to the bed.

'Ruy.' His name broke from her lips as he laid her down and she opened her eyes. Only then did she realise her arms were tight about his neck! In the lamplight his face was white and taut with emotion. Without a word he stumbled back, turned on his heel and left her.

CHAPTER EIGHT

YSANNE awoke to a bright, sunny room, without knowing how long she had slept. The monotonous chant of the indian women had droned on for hours until she had buried her head in the pillows in an attempt to stifle the noise. She had not undressed and still wore the gown in which she had been married.

Her dreams had been numerous. She had found herself running from Ruy on foot, through the Valle de Lágrimas, and each and every person she met turned away, unwilling to help her. Then Felipe, her own brother, was in pursuit of her, his face and clothes streaked with blood. Only Sancho offered her help, but she could never reach him. First a fire separated her from the hand outstretched to aid her, then Felipe blocked her path, smiling that hateful smile that made her instantly turn and run in the opposite direction.

There was a hand on her shoulder shaking her. She had begun to doze again. She started up, fearful of who might be confronting her. The relief which flooded over her when she found it was only Manuela was so enormous, she felt quite faint and slid down on to the pillows again, allowing herself to relax and overcome the unpleasant memories left by her disturbed night.

'Ysanne, are you all right?' Manuela asked in a

concerned tone. There was no sign of the distraught girl Ysanne had seen last night. 'I came to see if there was anything I could do for the new mistress of the house.'

Mistress of Pinos Altos! How that would have thrilled her six months ago, now it meant nothing. Liar, her heart cried, immediately forcing her to shut out all sentimental thoughts. Ruy had taken the decision to marry her and keep his word to her father as matter-of-factly as he did everything else. Once his mind had been made up, nothing could budge him from a determined course. No doubt in due course he would mention the Valle de Lágrimas. Believing that was her only defence against him, otherwise it would be so easy to accept the new role thrust upon her. Accept it, believe in him and offer her love, regardless of the fact that he would never return it. She would be a good wife. Had she not been trained by Tía Dolores herself?

'No, only tired,' she answered, raising herself up on to one elbow to regard the tray on the bedside table. 'This is very kind, Manuela.'

'Ruy,' the girl began hesitantly, 'he has told me you are his wife. How brave you are, Ysanne. After everything I told you, to come to him. How you must love him!'

Ysanne blinked at her tiredly and instantly the girl was contrite.

'I have awakened you too early, but Ruy's news was so wonderful, I had to come and congratulate you. Forgive me. Stay there and rest a while. I will tell Terecita to bring your breakfast up here.'

'No, you must not do that.' As much as the idea appealed to her Ysanne knew she had to go downstairs.

'I have good news too. The doctor is with Juan now and he is certain he will recover consciousness in a short while. I have been praying for him all night. I knew God would not be so cruel as to take him away from me.'

'Surely it was not God who tried to take him away—but Felipe,' Ysanne said, sitting bolt upright and Manuela sank down on to the edge of the bed with a gasp.

'You know? Ruy told you?'

'I want you to tell me. I know it must be very painful, but I have to know everything. Everything, do you hear, from the time I left you.'

Manuela stared at her, her lips beginning to tremble.

'We were almost to the waterhole when Felipe came upon us. He must have seen us approaching and waited. He ignored Juan at first and spoke only to me, telling me everything was going to be all right now, I must return with him to the Hacienda de las Flores and he would protect me against Juan. Of course I refused, but he wouldn't accept my answer. He said I was too afraid to speak of my true feelings with Juan beside me—and then he attacked him. He threw himself at Juan, dragged him from his horse and they began to fight. You know Juan is stronger, but something seemed to have possessed Felipe. He had the strength of ten men. He hit Juan with a rock. When I grabbed his arm to stop him hitting him again as he lay on the ground he grabbed me. I shall never forget the look in his eyes as he held me. Ysanne, I have never been so terrified in all my life. I thought Juan was dead . . . and he was going to kill me too . . . and then he began to kiss me . . .'

'Don't distress yourself further. I think I can guess what happened. You managed to break free, not without marking him with your nails, and rode home to get help?' Ysanne said, leaning forward to place an arm comfortingly around the girl's shoulders. What a dreadful experience! Manuela would forget in time, but Ysanne wondered if she ever would. Now she had undoubted proof of her brother's deception—his fanatical desire to have Manuela at all costs. He had almost killed Juan, was it not then possible he had killed his own father, and Pedro Valdez?

'How—how did you know?'

'I saw Felipe after he came home. I wish I had not.'

'Poor Ysanne. Your own brother. What can I say to ease your pain?'

'Dear Manuela, I should be saying that to you after all the grief and unpleasantness he has made for you and Juan—and Ruy. I must talk to him. It cannot wait any longer and he must give me answers.'

'He is asleep. He did not go to bed until after five this morning. I heard him come upstairs. I doubt if he will be down for breakfast.'

'But I will,' Ysanne assured her. Perhaps some food inside her might ease the awful hollow feeling in her stomach.

'Good. I will have Terecita lay another place.'

'Manuela, one more thing. Something Chato said last night, about men from Pinos Altos being murdered at the waterhole. I don't understand. I saw only one, a young boy.'

'Chato's son,' Manuela said, her young face grave. 'He has sworn a terrible vow of revenge against those who did it. Our men were there too, Ysanne. Dead too, but their bodies had been dragged behind some scrub bushes a few hundred yards away and Ruy did not find them for almost an hour. Our cattle are scattered. It could be days before they are found.'

Chato's son and the women who had gone to cook for the men—murdered!

'I shall need something to wear,' Ysanne said dully, refusing to allow her mind to dwell on who had committed these acts. 'A blouse and riding skirt will do. Nothing elaborate.'

'Those are hardly clothes fit for a bride, but if you are sure . . . ?'

Ysanne nodded and reached for the cup of coffee on the tray. Half an hour later she regarded her reflection in the mirror and a soft sigh escaped her. A white silk blouse and soft brown doeskin trousers, probably made by the indian women, who were experts at making such things. How often had she ridden at Ruy's side in such attire?

Hesitantly she came out of her room and turned in the direction of the stairs. The door of Juan's room opened and she heard voices as she approached, then Dr Sánchez stepped into view, quietly closing the door behind him.

'Doña Ysanne! I am surprised to see you here.'

'I—I came to be with Manuela the moment I heard Juan had had an accident,' Ysanne said. It was the easiest excuse she could think of and was apparently accepted. 'How is he this morning?'

'Showing signs of recovering consciousness, which will be a blessing. I don't like prolonged periods of unconsciousness after a head injury like the one he received. I've made it plain to Manuela he must be kept in bed for several days and watched at all times. If she is not happy with his condition, I am to be called back at once. Providing he has no ill-effects from the blow, he should be able to get up for short spells next week. Lucky young man, Juan. He almost met with the same kind of accident as his father. Riding the same horse, so Ruy told me, which probably explains it. I'd have the brute put down if it was mine.'

'The injury to his head was similar?' Ysanne heard herself asking and praying he would not give her the answer she was expecting.

'Almost identical. Thrown, I'd say. Nasty piece of horseflesh in my opinion. See if you can make the boy get rid of it.'

Ysanne watched him go downstairs, followed at a distance. The same injury as his father. The words hammered at her brain. Felipe had hit Juan with a rock. Manuela had seen it! So the death of Pedro Valdez had not been an accident. The signs of another horse which Juan had seen had probably belonged to Felipe, making his way home. Another reason for him to be silenced. He had seen the tracks! He knew his father had not died accidentally.

The dining-room to the left of the staircase was empty. She went in and sat down. Almost immediately, Terecita, the Navajo housekeeper, materialised from a side room and placed in front of her a huge plate containing bacon, eggs and freshly smoked ham accompanied by hot buttered toast and more steaming hot coffee. Did she look as if she needed fattening, Ysanne wondered, as she did her best to wade through everything. The woman did not speak to her. She would not under the circumstances, she thought. Her grandson was dead at the hands of the brother of the girl she served. Yet there was no hostility in her face, nor in her voice, as she cleared away some time later and politely enquired if the señora wished for anything else. Ysanne said she did not. She wanted only to talk to Ruy. She was wondering what to do with herself until he awoke, when he came into the room, water still glistening on his black hair. Rolling back the sleeves of his shirt over berry-brown arms, he sat down and was immediately presented with an even larger meal than Ysanne had been given.

'You slept well?' He looked across at her as he reached for his coffee. She could see nothing in him now of the man who had kissed her so ruthlessly and with such passion the night before.

'Not really. There was too much to think about.'

'Put it out of your head. For you it's over.'

'I won't accept that. Manuela told me what really happened to Juan. Felipe's story was the exact opposite.'

'You didn't tell me you had spoken to Felipe?' He stared at her, his breakfast still untouched. 'You saw him come home?'

'*Sí*. He was bloody and covered in scratches. He lied, of course. I knew it as soon as he began to tell me what happened.' Without wanting to, she found herself telling him of Manuela's visit and the conclusions she had reached once she had left the house. He listened in silence. She waited, expecting condemnation or recriminations, but he said nothing and started on his breakfast without answering her.

'Are you not going to say something? Tell me how right you were and how stupid I am?' she flung the words across the table at him, unable to stand the agony of silence.

'What good will that do?' He shrugged broad shoulders. 'You know what Felipe is now, that's all that matters. When Juan is strong enough I am taking him into the town to lay charges of attempted murder against your brother. After that it is up to the court and a judge. Nothing you can say or do will change my mind, so don't try. Manuela has persuaded me that is the only right way to do things. If I had my way I'd kill him and save a lot of good people time and money trying him.'

'Señor Ruy, we have company.' Chato stood in the doorway. He ignored Ysanne. 'Sancho Morales and four men are coming up the main trail. They are alone, we have checked.'

'Bring them into the *sala*. I will speak to them there,' Ruy said and continued eating, apparently unconcerned.

'What does he want?' Ysanne gasped in alarm.

'His bride perhaps?'

The taunt struck home and brought fierce colour into her cheeks. With as much dignity as she could muster she rose to her feet.

'Am I allowed to speak with him or not? It might be better, or do you want more trouble?'

'I am prepared for it, although I do not think he is the kind of man who would be so foolish as to provoke me in my own house. More likely Felipe has sent him,' Ruy returned indifferently. 'Very well. You may receive him before I see him, but I warn you Ysanne, play me false . . . Felipe is a murderer, a liar and a thief. I am determined he will not kill again to have the Valle de Lágrimas.'

Ysanne halted in the doorway, her face pale

now. She knew the next few minutes were going to be the most difficult of her life. She had to tell Sancho of her suspicions, her doubts and her fears. As a judge he would be better able to weigh them up carefully and methodically. She was too emotionally involved. One tiny straw and she would still clutch at it hoping Felipe's innocence could be proved.

'You are wrong, Ruy. He does not want that. I thought you might have guessed by now. He wants—and has always wanted—only Manuela.'

With that parting shot she left him sitting stock still as if he had been struck by a thunderbolt.

'Thank you, Terecita.' Ysanne forced a smile to her lips as the woman put down a tray of coffee on the table beside her, brought up a decanter of wine and two glasses and placed those near at hand. 'Will you bring another glass, my husband will be joining us in a moment.'

In the chair opposite Sancho's face registered disbelief, then strangely enough, resignation, at her words, delivered without warning of any kind.

'When did this happen?' His voice was perfectly controlled, in no way betraying the jolt her announcement must surely have given him.

'Last night.'

'He forced you to agree?'

'No. Why should he? You know how I feel about him. Have always felt. I am so sorry, Sancho. I did write to you. When you came to dinner on Saturday I intended to tell you we could never marry, make you accept it. You never have in the past. Ruy did force my hand insomuch as he came to the house and fetched me. He was worried for my safety.'

'The woman Serafina said you went of your own free will, but Felipe insisted you had been abducted. What do you mean, Ruy was worried for your safety?'

'Will you take coffee or wine, Sancho?'

'Wine, and stop fencing. I want to know what is going on.'

'Very well, but you will like it no more than I did. If only you will believe what I am about to tell you and stop more killing. Unless you do, my brother is going to turn Ruy into a murderer like himself.'

She poured him a glass of wine and he took it in silence, watching with a fierce frown as she poured coffee for herself, sipped it and then put it aside, in obvious agitation.

Ysanne spared herself nothing. She began at the very beginning when she had returned home, what she had seen, her reception at the *hacienda* and the incident in the study. The plans she and Felipe had made for the protection of their home and lands, his strangeness which grew as the weeks passed, his obsession for Manuela. The pain and grief of those weeks flooded back, but she kept her composure and did not falter. She could not! The only thing she kept from him was the truth of her relationship with Ruy. She would have to deal with that sometime in the future, but just now it took second place to other, more important things.

When she had finished, she sat back in her chair, pale-faced, drained, suddenly afraid. Sancho rose, poured out a large glass of wine and pressed it into her cold hands.

'Drink,' he ordered and she obeyed without a word. He took the glass and sat down again, his eyes intent on her face.

'I have some questions. Do you feel up to answering them?'

'Of course. Ask me anything.'

'These letters you say Ruy wrote to you? What could have happened to them?'

'Either he never wrote them, which I now believe is not the truth, or someone—someone else has them.'

'Felipe? *Sí*, it would suit his purpose to keep you and Ruy apart. I suspected I was being used, but this old heart was determined to have you, Ysanne. I was foolish and blind.'

'Don't say that,' she whispered contritely. 'All this is still supposition. It has to be proved—I don't think it is going to be possible.'

'The will then? What has happened to that?'

'Father said he was going to make out a new one in my favour, but I don't know if he ever did. I only know what he told me before he went away. I thought he had changed his mind because Felipe had been such a help to him after his first illness. I did not care.'

'You should have. If he did make a second will, what did he do with it? Does Felipe have it along with Ruy's letters.'

'I should say that is a fair assumption of the situation,' Ruy said, coming unannounced into the room. Noting the extra glass on the table he poured himself some wine. His eyes were questioning as he looked down at Ysanne, but his words were addressed to Sancho.

'What brings you here at this early hour?'

'Felipe has accused Juan of trying to kill him. He had to be talked out of bringing all the men from the ranch here and raiding this place.'

'That would have been very foolish of him, although it might also have saved me the trouble of going looking for him if the courts fail to give me justice,' Ruy returned, leaning against a sideboard. 'Has Ysanne told you what happened—her version, I mean.'

'She had given me a most detailed description of what Felipe looked like when he returned home. Her testimony in court will be invaluable.'

'That will not be necessary,' Ruy intervened harshly. 'She is not to be called as a witness. I do not want her further involved in all this.'

'If you wish to prove that Felipe is behind all this trouble, then she will be a prime witness,' Sancho said, glowering in his direction. Ysanne had never seen him angry before. He was quite formidable. So, too, was Ruy, as he straightened.

'He is her brother. Good God, man, don't you think she has been through enough? To discover what he is? It's eating her heart out. I won't have it go on.'

'I think I am the best one to answer Sancho's question,' Ysanne said quietly. 'If he brings me proof—undisputable proof—that Felipe is behind everything, then I will testify. I will testify, because you will have proved that my brother murdered his own father. I could forgive him many things, protect him out of love, loyalty, stupidity even. But I will not shield the man who killed my father—no matter who it is.'

'We should talk,' Ruy said to Sancho and she rose to her feet, knowing she was not expected to stay.

'I will see you again before you leave,' she said and Sancho nodded, with a smile. How his eyes ached with the pain she had given him this morning! Poor Sancho, he did not deserve it. He had been a good, kind friend. She looked at her husband, stated firmly, 'I am going for a walk. Call me when Sancho leaves, please.'

Detain me and he will know I have lied, her expression warned. He nodded and she left the room, feeling as if she had achieved a major triumph. She belonged to him, but he did not own her, could not dictate to her. Somehow she gained little pleasure from the knowledge.

'She is a very brave girl,' Sancho murmured as the door closed behind her. 'Felipe's rages have always mystified me. Now, I think, I begin to understand. She has risked much to be with you, but then, that was how it was meant to be, was it not? I tried to win her a thousand ways and she would not have me. Only you! Only Ruy Valdez was meant for Ysanne de Rivas. She made you sound like a prince in shining armour. I offered her everything I had and she wanted none of it. A brave girl. I hope you appreciate what you have gained.'

'I am beginning to realise I have gained more than I thought.' Ruy filled their glasses and seated himself in the chair Ysanne had vacated. 'Let us be serious now, Sancho. There is much I have to tell you . . .'

The sun was warm on Ysanne's back as she strolled away from the house, towards the tall pine trees stretching upwards in the distance. She had walked here many times. She knew many of the back trails and the sentries on watch ignored her presence. She realised she was still trembling. It had begun the moment she started to talk of Felipe to Sancho.

What if she was wrong? No, she could not be. Too many things had happened and they could not all be coincidence.

'Señora.' The voice came off from her right. She stopped, but could see no one. 'Here, señora.'

A man materialised from the bushes, a rifle in one hand, and she stared at him suspiciously. Had Ruy sent him to watch her?

'Is it true the señora would like to go home? Back to the Hacienda de las Flores?'

Her heartbeats quickened. She was being offered a way of escape. Was this a trap? Then, in the wake of the sudden excitement, came caution. Why should she leave? If everything Ruy said was true, her life would be in danger if she returned home. She had stated her intention of being a witness against Felipe if the charges against him were proved. She was dangerous to him! Her steps faltered. She tried to go to one side of the man, but he stepped in front of her, blocking her path.

'I am one of your brother's men. Trust me. I can get you out of here tonight,' he insisted.

She looked into the narrowed eyes, the surly, tanned face, and was afraid. One of Felipe's men? But he worked for Ruy!

'I do not know you,' she said in a hollow tone.

'You would not. You will have to trust me. Tonight, after dinner, come out to the stables. I will be waiting. I will get you safely home.'

'How can you work for my brother when you are in the employ of Ruy Valdez?'

She knew the question was a mistake the moment it was uttered. The man's eyes narrowed even more and the lean lips tightened into a forbidding line. What had she stumbled on here? Men working for Felipe and at the same time working for Ruy? Men willing to betray one master for another?

'How else does your brother get his dirty work done?' His words stunned her. Suddenly she was imagining the waterhole, with men from both *ranchos* sitting at ease, the women cooking, and then friends were pulling guns and shooting down men they had known perhaps for years, women they had slept with, a young boy they had taught to ride at an early age, as a friend would! It was unbelievable, yet believable! It was the answer! The horror which leapt to her eyes betrayed the fact she knew nothing. The man swore vilely and she turned to run. He was upon her in an instant, restraining hands pinioning her arms to her sides. 'Be still! Quiet!' he ordered. 'You are coming with me now. Don Felipe will pay much to get you back, and when I tell him what a fuss you made . . .'

'No!' Ysanne screamed the word at him. A clumsy hand fumbled to close around her mouth. She sank her teeth into his fingers and he swore at her, cuffed her viciously with his clenched hand and she reeled backwards on to the ground. He followed her down, apparently enjoying the feel of her young body struggling against his. She saw something else mirrored in his eyes, a desire that appalled her, made her fight that much more fiercely against his determination to master her.

'You always were a high and mighty little madam,' he said, as his lips sought hers. 'When I've finished with you, Ruy Valdez can have what's left and your brother won't have to worry about a traitor.'

He had somehow overheard her conversation with Sancho, she realised. She felt her blouse tear and screamed, just once, before a blow across the face rendered her almost unconscious. His hands were moving over her bare flesh. She felt sick, but revived enough to scratch at his cheeks. As Manuela must have done with Felipe, was the last thought she remembered. His weight was suffocating her. She could not breathe. Her senses reeled . . . she gulped in clean air and screamed again and again. The sound echoed in her brain . . .

'Ysanne! Look at me. Ysanne, open your eyes.'

Sancho's voice. No, that was not possible. Yes, it was, he had come to Pinos Altos. She felt bruised in every limb. Wincing, she opened her eyes and tried to sit up, but the effort was too painful. It was Sancho's face hovering above hers, anxious and strained. She tried to speak, but no words would come, instead came only tears. She heard a groan and looked around. His knuckles bruised and bleeding, Ruy stood over the man who had attacked her.

'No,' she said faintly and he turned in her direction immediately.

'Are you all right?' His arms were about her and Sancho surrendered her into the care of the other man with a half-smile. She was Ruy's wife, after all.

'He—he spoke of working for Felipe . . . he wanted to take me home . . .' her voice was so faint he scarcely heard it. 'Felipe has men here—your men! You must find them.'

'First I get you back to the house,' Ruy said and she allowed herself to be lifted in his arms without a word. How strong they were, making her feel safe! When she opened her eyes again she was in her own room and Manuela was trying to get her out of her torn clothes. She allowed herself to be undressed without really knowing what was happening. Her head hurt and one arm where she had been thrown to the ground. She drifted in and out of sleep for hours. And then became aware of the fact someone was beside her. Fearfully she started up, but it was Ruy's gentle hands that rested on her shoulders, pressed her back on to the pillows.

'Hush, there is nothing to fear. We have the man and another six who worked with him. Worked for Felipe.'

'I—I was not dreaming? He has men here?'

'*Sí*. How else could he have attacked the villages of our *ranchos* so successfully? You have given me the answer to many questions, Ysanne. Sleep now.'

She turned her head away from him, tears scalding her cheeks. Proof of Felipe's guilt! Provided by his own sister!

'I am not proud of what I have done,' she whispered tearfully.

'Can I do nothing to ease your grief?' His voice was tender, sympathetic. 'Ysanne, look at me?'

She could not, but he turned her head and made her do so. Such a look in those dark eyes! He caught her to him as a muffled sob escaped her lips. She shuddered just once in his embrace and then was still, so still, he drew back and looked down into the face streaked with tears, the wide eyes, innocent and frightened. He was waiting for her to make the first move, she realised. She could not. Too much had happened between them. She had accused him of murder! Fingers, light as a breath of wind, shakily touched his cheek, his mouth. He did not move. It was as if he was made of stone.

'Do I not please you, Ruy Valdez? My aunt will be disappointed, she thought me a good pupil.'

She heard a soft curse explode under his breath and his arms tightened around her. His lips lightly touched her cheek and then her mouth. He was demanding nothing, but waiting for her to give. To prove her love! Her body ached from the unprovoked attack upon it, ached too for the arms of the man she loved to enfold it, caress it! She was committed. She had been since the day she returned home! Her fingers wound themselves in his thick hair and drew his head down to hers. Her mouth touched his, gingerly, apprehensively, and then it was like the igniting of a flame between them. A flame someone had sought to extinguish and failed and in their failure they had made the flame stronger, more durable. His hands were on her body and suddenly there was no pain, no bruising, only the sensation of giving and being fulfilled by the giving. Contentment! Love! It was all she had ever asked.

The next morning at breakfast she was surprised to see that Sancho was still with them. Ruy was gone by the time she awoke and for a while she had lingered in bed, hoping he would return and they could talk, but he did not. Had he accepted her love, or taken it as a matter of right? Manuela had come to her rescue again, with a dress this time, and she came downstairs hesitantly, not knowing how her husband would receive her after her boldness of the previous night.

As she came into the room Sancho immediately pulled out a chair for her and she seated herself with a smile.

'Not disappointed to see me still here, I hope?' he asked with a teasing smile.

'Sancho, don't be so horrid! We shared a very pleasant relationship. Why must it change? I never said or did anything to encourage you, did I?'

'No, you were always honest about your feelings for Ruy. Don't worry, nothing has changed. I want you to promise me, if you ever need help—of any kind—you will call on me at once,' he insisted.

'I will. I promise. Thank you. Is that the time?' Ysanne stared across at a mantel clock in surprise. 'Eleven o'clock! I seem to have been sleeping ever since I got here. Time has just slipped away.'

'Yesterday must have been very unpleasant for you. Nature has its own way of taking care of such things,' Sancho assured her. 'Ruy said you were sleeping like a baby when he left you earlier this morning. I think he was somewhat relieved you had managed to sleep. It was better you did anyway.'

'Why? What has happened? Juan is not worse?' Terecita arrived with another enormous breakfast. Ysanne gazed at it in dismay, it was far more than she usually ate, but the memory of the last time and the delicious taste of the food, made her simply smile and the woman went away satisfied.

'Last night Ruy attempted to question the men— the traitors among his workforce. It was not pleasant. You would not have enjoyed it. At times his temper could match that of Felipe.'

'No,' she said quietly, sipping her coffee. 'Felipe's anger and moods are something quite different from ordinary bouts of temper. I realise that now and that is what frightens me.'

'Surely you are out of his reach if you fear him that much. He cannot harm you here.' Sancho looked at her puzzledly.

'You do not understand my meaning. It—it is

difficult for me to explain . . . Madness, was how Ruy once described his temper. If my brother is mad, Sancho, what does that make me?'

'My dear child, there is no question . . .'

'But there is. Why should Felipe's blood be tainted and not mine? Perhaps it is, perhaps mine will show itself soon? I have begun to think of this so often lately.'

'Enough, Ysanne. You are as sane as I am,' Sancho interrupted, his kindly face rather pale. 'There is nothing wrong with you.'

'Will I ever be able to prove it?' Her voice broke and she forced herself to begin eating from the plate in front of her. 'Did Ruy learn anything from the men? The one who attacked me?'

'Nothing. They are more frightened of Felipe than of what can happen to them either here or in a court of law. I, too, begin to wonder about your brother's state of mind, Ysanne. They keep silent, not out of loyalty, but fear! Real fear! I saw their faces.'

'Then we are lost. Without their testimony what can we prove? It may make Ruy impatient to finish what is between Felipe and him. That must not happen.'

'It will not. The law will take its course. Once Juan has laid charges against Felipe, we will proceed from there.'

'And if he lays a counter-claim?'

'Both have to be proved—or disproved,' Sancho said gravely. 'The weeks ahead are not going to be pleasant for you, you realise that, don't you? You have said you will testify and I am relying on that. If you come forward, maybe others will too. One way or the other we will find out who is at the bottom of these killings and the destruction. Are you prepared for—anything?'

'You mean Felipe being proved innocent and Ruy in his place?' Ysanne asked falteringly. '*Sí*, I have considered that. If you had seen the way my brother looked, listened to him as he spoke of Manuela . . . I am not wrong, Sancho. My love for Ruy has not blinded me. In fact it kept me away from him too long. My love for my brother blinded me, made me deaf to what was said about him, what he might have become. Believe me, I am prepared for anything.'

'I told him you were brave. How I envy him what he now possesses.'

'Sancho, please. If you continue to talk that way, we cannot remain friends. You will make it too difficult and believe me, I do want—need—your friendship.'

'You have it, my dear, but for a while at least, you must allow me to indulge in a little self-pity. The loser always does. Eat your food before it gets cold.'

Later, as they sat on the verandah drinking coffee before Sancho left, Ysanne was disturbed more than once by the sound of shouting coming from one of the barns. No, not quite shouting . . . more an agonised cry, quickly muffled. Sancho appeared not to notice whenever she looked in his direction, but once, when she caught him unawares, she saw he was alert, listening to every sound. Almost anticipating.

Ruy came striding from the direction of the sounds as she gathered courage to ask what was happening. Joining them, he flung himself into a chair, a tight smile tugging at his lips.

'You have the proof you want, *amigo*. All of it. Go and listen.'

As Sancho left them without a word, Ysanne could contain her questions no longer.

'You—are you torturing those men to make them speak?'

'No. I am doing nothing. They are in Chato's care. They killed his son. I did not think I had the right to deny him the answers to a few questions.'

'What is he doing to them?' she gasped.

'Ysanne, your imagination is running wild. He has taken the Navajo women in there with him. A few descriptions on what they can do to a man and I guarantee any tongue will be loosened. The women took their knives with them. A formidable bunch they looked too, and quite serious in what they intended to do if someone did not talk.'

'You—you could not allow that to happen?'

'Have you forgotten your first day home? The man that was killed? What about the waterhole? Women shot from behind? Chato's son? I am done with weakness, Ysanne. Sit down, they are not going to be cut to pieces. A few little cuts here and there is nothing compared to what they have done for your brother over the past months. They have to talk to Sancho. Then it is done. I will take them into town and hand them over to the sheriff in a day or two. I want them to sweat a little. Know fear as their victims have.' Ruy poured himself coffee, drank it straight down and then went inside, returning with a full glass of whisky. He looked down at her questioningly, but she did not pursue the conversation. His methods were cruel to her, but the ends justified the means . . . and she was sure the Navajo women would not harm any one of the men without his explicit order. She knew that would never be given. He was not Felipe.

She made an attempt at lighter conversation.

'Manuela is going to run out of clothes if I keep borrowing them. Will you ask Sancho to arrange for my own things to be sent from the house. I would like Serafina with me too.'

'*Sí*. I should like a long talk with that old dragon who listens at keyholes,' he returned with a nod of approval. The dress she wore was plain, yet he thought how beautiful she looked. She needed no frills or fripperies to enhance what nature had endowed her with. Why had she thought she did? Had it really been his fault? Had he really been so indifferent to her? She had shared his company and many things he would have refused even other young men of his own age. The intimate moments when they had just sat together, watching the sun go down after riding in the high country for most of the day, or swam at the waterhole after herding in the cattle to drink and graze for the day. Now, he realised, her thoughts had been far different from his. A husband, and a family! For the scraggy, tousle-haired girl who rode at his side, could track almost as well as Juan, light a fire and prepare a meal out in the open with the most primitive of utensils. She had been growing up right under his nose and he had noticed it too late, because by the time he knew what he wanted—she had gone to Monterey.

Would she believe him if he told her, or think he was merely being kind after what had happened between them? So much was happening, he found himself unable to give himself completely yet, to accept the marvel she was offering, without reservations—without self-condemnation for his own blindness! In time perhaps—if nothing else happened to part them as it had once before.

He knew she was watching him, waiting for him to say something which would set her mind, her heart, at rest. He could not find the words.

'I think Sancho should have satisfied himself as to the guilt of your brother by now,' he said, rising, and the genuine disappointment which registered on her face cut him like a knife. 'I will ask him to arrange for your clothes to be sent here. The woman too. Anything else?'

Much more, Ysanne thought miserably, but only you can give it to me and you refuse me even that small gesture.

'No, I need nothing else.'

CHAPTER NINE

THREE days had elapsed since Ysanne had been abducted from her home and brought to Pinos Altos. Sancho had come and gone. The men who worked for her brother, betraying the trust Ruy had placed in them, were still prisoners in one of the barns. Juan had recovered consciousness, and despite doctor's orders and Manuela's entreaties, had insisted on coming downstairs to sit on the verandah and be with the rest of the family. She was part of that family now. Ruy's wife, but for one night only. He had not come to her again and she had fallen asleep, waiting for him to do so.

Juan's story had not differed from the one she had already been told. Felipe had met them on their way home, tried to talk with Manuela and when he had failed, turned on her companion in a blind fury. He had sent her riding home to fetch help, and had remembered nothing until he recovered again at Pinos Altos. Ysanne was grateful his attitude towards her had not changed. She had been so afraid he would blame her for the actions of her brother.

Ruy's attitude towards her was very cool. Polite, but distant, and she was certain he went out of his way to ensure they spent very little time alone together. Where he slept at night she did not know and she was too hurt to ask. She had been rejected.

His promise to her father was all that had mattered to him—not her! Or the love she offered.

'Ysanne, help me, I can't manage him alone,' Manuela said breathlessly. She was standing by the verandah steps, one of Juan's arms around her shoulders. He was exceedingly pale and breathing heavily. She had been so lost in thought she had not seen them approach.

'Give me your other arm, Juan. You look exhausted. You are doing too much, you know.' Together the two young women managed to get him up on to the verandah and into a chair. 'A little stimulant, I think, Manuela. Brandy, but not too much.'

'I deserve a large glass for my efforts this morning.' Juan gave her a cheeky grin, but it was obvious he had used up all his strength. 'It's no use looking at me like that, or Manuela giving me one of her lectures. I have to get back on my feet and get into town. Heavens knows what Felipe is cooking up while I sit here doing nothing. And we have to get those men out of here, they are a potential danger to us all. I wouldn't put it past him to try and get them free. He is crazy enough, even though he knows he will be outnumbered and outgunned. I almost wish he would, I'd like a chance to get back at him . . .' he broke off as Ysanne stepped back from him. 'I'm sorry, but you can't blame me, can you?'

'No, but he is still my brother, Juan. The pain I feel now will not go easily—if ever,' she said quietly.

'He is a danger to us all while he remains unchallenged,' Juan insisted. 'To Manuela, me, you and Ruy. He would like to see us all dead.'

'Who would?' Ruy asked, coming out to join them. 'What have you been doing with yourself this morning? I tell you to stay in bed and rest and you are up almost as soon as I am. Terecita tells me you hardly ate anything for breakfast.'

'I promised her she could give me a large meal tonight. Don't treat me like a little boy, Ruy. I know what is at stake for us all. Without me, you can trust only Chato, until we have checked out the story those men gave us. Do you think I haven't heard you wandering about at night, inspecting our defences, watching the sentries. Poor Ysanne, what a honeymoon she is having. No husband. Just a watchdog. Another day and I think I could cope with being taken into town in the wagon. No, don't argue, I have made up my mind. I hurt Ysanne just now by saying I would like to get back at Felipe for what he has done to us. That goes for you too, I know. The longer we wait on my account, the more chance he has of persuading people you did kidnap Ysanne and force her into marriage with you to get control of the valley. He can be very persuasive, as you know. Even Sancho may not be able to swing the tide of opinion in our favour.'

'If—if you wish me to go into town with you, I will,' Ysanne said in a hollow tone and Ruy looked at her sharply, 'but I will not lie. I will only tell what I know and have seen. That amounts to very little.'

'You have seen the way Felipe looks sometimes, especially when he is hurting someone,' Juan interrupted grimly. 'As I have. We know what he is capable of, Ysanne.'

'No. She does not come with us. If you really feel up to it, you and I will take half-a-dozen men and take the prisoners into town tomorrow afternoon.

We will go through the high country until we are almost out of the valley. That way we should avoid Felipe's patrol. It is there every day.'

'That is not nearly enough men,' Manuela protested. 'You have seven prisoners. What if they try to escape. Take more.'

'If I did, I would leave Pinos Altos virtually unprotected,' Ruy returned tersely. 'I have men watching the waterhole, men watching the patrol, men here guarding the trails to the house. They are stretched out thinly as it is. Chato will stay to protect you. If there is trouble, he has enough skill to get you away before any of Felipe's men get here. We have already discussed a plan of action.'

'He—he would not come here,' Manuela breathed and Ysanne saw she was clearly terrified of the thought.

He might, she thought, but did not put her fear into words. For Manuela she suspected Felipe would do anything, risk anything—even his life. She was his life! She saw Ruy watching her and knew the same thought was in his mind too. Why would he not take her with him? Was he afraid that, faced with the test, she would not go through with it and remain silent, refusing to testify on Juan's behalf? Could he think so little of her?

Manuela was urging Juan to rest and eventually he gave in to her pleas. Alone with Ruy, Ysanne at once felt uncomfortable and turned to go also, but he stopped her.

'Don't run away. By the look of the dust cloud approaching, this is what you have been expecting.'

She turned back, not understanding, watching the heavy pall of dust which hung low in the sky, settling over nearby trees. Into view came a wagon, driven at a fast pace. Clinging to her seat was the enormous frame of Serafina, bouncing up and down like a rubber ball as the vehicle hit uneven ground. Ysanne heard her wail of disapproval even over the loud drumming of the horses hoofs. As the driver drew rein in front of the verandah she fell out into Ruy's outstretched arms, her face a picture of misery.

'Every bone in my body is broken,' she moaned. 'This fool tried to kill me. Don't give him sanctuary. Send him back to Don Felipe. They deserve each other.'

'Serafina, what on earth has happened to you?' Ysanne felt an awful urge to laugh at the woman's discomfort. Serafina, she knew of old, was a tyrant where other servants were concerned, always thinking herself above them because she was the personal maid and confidante of the mistress of the house. She looked like a beggar woman now. Her dress and face were streaked with dirt. Her hair hung down her back in the most unkempt fashion and looked as if it had not been touched in days. The smile faded from her face. She went to her, relieved Ruy of the sagging bulk and helped her up to a chair. 'Felipe—he did not dare . . .'

'*Sí*. He dared. You would not believe what the house has been like since he,' she cast a baleful glare at Ruy, 'took you away. *Dios mío*, that one was fathered by the devil himself.'

'Serafina, you forget yourself. I will forgive you because you are upset.'

'Let her speak. This woman is your closest friend, an ally, and Felipe has always known it. Let her tell us how she was treated when you were not there to protect her,' Ruy intervened, hooking out a chair beside them and sitting down. 'Tell us everything from the time I took your mistress. Everything!'

'He came back in the early hours. He went to bed without knowing you had gone. I did not tell him. I wanted to give you time to get here safely.'

'You allowed me to be taken from my home against my will,' Ysanne said angrily. 'If my brother remonstrated with you for this, then he was perfectly right to do so. You should have raised the alarm when you had the chance.'

'And deprived you of a safe haven, *mi niña*? A man who had sworn to your own father to look after you, no matter how he had to do it, no matter what you thought of him if the circumstances were beyond his control?' Serafina looked into Ysanne's pale features, wiped the dust from her mouth and then looked back at the driver of the wagon who still sat in his seat. 'I did not mean what I said. Don Felipe only sent him because he is no longer of use. His son was killed at the waterhole and he has no other family. When Don Felipe asked for a volunteer to drive me here, he did not expect anyone to be so bold as to agree. For his boldness he gave that man ten lashes. Not personally, of course, but he watched and made everyone else do so too.'

Ruy sprang from his seat and leaped down the stairs to the wagon, calling for men to come and help him. She watched in silence as the driver was helped away to one of the bunk-houses. Whipped? Because he had been brave enough—or foolish enough to drive Serafina to Pinos Altos? He had not changed. He was still as unpredictable, dangerous, untrustworthy as he had been in childhood.

Perhaps more dangerous now. And devious.

'Did my brother really have him beaten?' She whispered.

'*Sí*, he did.'

'And you, Serafina. What did he do to you. Don Sancho said you told him I had left of my own free will. Did you not realise my brother would never believe such a thing?'

'You would be surprised what he believes,' Serafina said with a shrug of her shoulders. 'At first he called me a liar and called on Señor Morales to gather men from both the ranch and his own home to come here and kill Don Ruy. The Señor refused, of course. He is not a fool. He loves you, but he is a cautious man. A good man. He sensed something was wrong. I told him everything that had happened, except that I pretended you had accompanied Don Ruy willingly. I wanted no more blood spilled. Your father smiled on me that night. I could almost hear him saying, "well done, Serafina. You protect her as well as you did when she was little." What Don Felipe did to me afterwards was of small consequence.'

'What did he do, woman?' Ruy stood behind her chair, his face taut with anger. 'Did you not have enough sense to lie and save yourself from punishment?'

'Lie? Had I done so, Pinos Altos would have been attacked by over a hundred men. Don Felipe talked of riding into town and rousing all Ysanne's friends. You knew what you were doing when you took her, señor, but did you weigh the consequences carefully?'

'Every one. I expected you to tell Felipe what he wanted to hear. I trusted Sancho in his wisdom to hold back any ill feeling until I could get Juan to town.'

'You must do so as soon as possible,' Serafina insisted. 'Her brother's tongue is smooth, already he has gained support from many people. Don Sancho may have trouble controlling the high feelings of some of them, especially as many of them remember what was said the day Don Diego was buried. To them, Felipe is a poor lost young man who has lost his father and now his sister, abducted by the very man she has accused of murdering her father.' Serafina's eyes held tears as they turned on Ysanne. 'It was a bad day when you spoke those words, *mi niña*. You condemned him before everyone—and you knew nothing.'

'It seems I still do not.' Ysanne sprang to her feet, her cheeks flushed with bright colour. How dare the pair of them sit in judgment of her. 'I spoke words from my heart. I meant every one of them.'

'So the other night was a lie,' Ruy drawled softly and she sank back into her seat, lost for words. 'I hope it was worth the effort you put into it.'

Her hand flashed out to strike at his face, but he easily averted the intended blow, and said coldly,

'Sit still and listen. I think she has more to tell us.'

'I was locked in my room. One of the maids brought me water and bread, but that is all I have been allowed in three days.' Ysanne gasped and instantly began to rise to her feet to call Terecita and have some food prepared, but Ruy waved her to be still and reluctantly she was so. 'I could hear your brother's voice for most of the first night, ranting at Don Sancho. Then, after he had gone, Don Felipe went to town. He came back rejoicing at the support he had received and got very drunk. That was a blessing, he did not come near me. The next day he told me I was free to come to you, but I would be allowed to bring nothing with me. I could stay with him, he said, substantiate his story that you had been abducted and he would reward me well. When I refused, he had all my furniture taken from my room, along with my clothes, and burned in the courtyard. I was made to watch. Then he asked for a man to drive the wagon here. Everyone knew what would happen if he volunteered, but Estebán did. With his son dead he no longer cared what happened to him. He is a good man, señor,' she said to Ruy. 'Care for him. He will work hard for you.'

'I will,' he assured her. 'Go on.'

'He made me take out all the señorita's dresses, her shoes, her most precious possessions.' Tears now streamed down over Serafina's plum cheeks. '*Mi niña*, he has left you nothing. You have two trunks full of rags, broken ornaments, anything you cared for he has destroyed. Even the beautiful decanters you brought back for your father are smashed and his collection of jade, most of which you gave him . . .'

'Did Felipe do—this—himself?' Ysanne somehow forced the words out.

'*Sí*. This he wanted to enjoy personally.'

As if in a dream, Ysanne went down to the wagon. One of the *vaqueros* had unloaded the trunks. She knelt on the ground, her skirt trailing unnoticed in inches of dirt and fumbled with trembling fingers to open the lid of one of them. Inside this one was what was left of her day dresses and ball gowns. Each and every one she lifted out had been systematically shredded with a knife. She could salvage nothing from the destruction which faced her. She felt sick! Felipe had done this? Why? Because he knew she had deserted him in her heart, whatever she said to the contrary? Because he had lost an ally? A pawn? Because he had lost the advantage over Ruy when she became his wife? That was more like the real reason, but there was more. Something deeper, more terrible and she could not put her finger on it. He was different yet she knew he could not be. They both shared the same mother and father. The thought that their blood might be tainted terrified her. Her children would inherit that trait!

Someone was behind her, lifting her gently, but firmly to her feet. It was her husband. She shrank from his touch with her thoughts still vivid in her mind and he released her with a frown.

'I will have these taken upstairs or disposed of, whichever you prefer. When I am in town, perhaps you would like to have me do some shopping for you?'

'What do I need here? Would you appreciate fine silks and satins? I doubt it. Pinos Altos is all you care for. I want nothing. *Sí*, have them taken upstairs. Serafina, come and help me. Terecita can bring you something in my room. You shall sleep in the room next to mine tonight and try to forget what has happened.'

'Will you be able to?' Ruy asked stonily as she turned away. He watched her shoulders straighten defiantly and without a word she strode into the house. Serafina hesitated. He nodded and she followed, her face registering a mixture of displeasure and puzzlement.

Half an hour later, sitting with Chato on the verandah, a bottle of brandy between them, Ruy said moodily,

'Tomorrow afternoon we go into town. Juan travels in the wagon. You stay here to guard the women. I'll take a dozen men. Bring in some from the waterhole and leave the same number on the trail. I don't trust Felipe. He may try anything.'

'Why not take the women along?' Chato looked at his friend and employer and thought it had been a long time since he had seen him so disturbed in his mind. Don Felipe de Rivas or his wife, he wondered? He refilled both glasses and tossed his back without appreciation. He never did understand the great need for brandy among white men when they could have a home-brew just as potent. He would go to the women afterwards, there was always a jug there and he could try to forget the son he had just laid to rest.

'No. I have many reasons, none of which you would understand. Manuela is not strong, Chato, she would panic and be a liability if we were attacked. My—wife,' the hesitation was not lost on the other man, 'I have to prove beyond all doubt that her brother is what I say he is. She loves him. She will always have her doubts unless . . .'

'She is your woman. She should obey you.'

'It is not that simple, not with a fire-brand like Ysanne. There will never be anyone else like her.'

'That is good?'

'For me it could be very bad. We are too much alike, kindred spirits. And we both have hellish tempers when roused. I can see no future for us. When this is over it would be better if I let her go. She will have the Hacienda de las Flores, the Valle de Lágrimas, she will be a wealthy woman in her own right . . .'

'And still your wife,' he was reminded.

Ruy grimaced and picked up his glass.

'*Salud, amigo!* Let's finish the bottle. Who knows what tomorrow may bring.'

Ysanne refused to go to bed. She had had Terecita bring up some food for Serafina and ordered the room next to hers to be prepared and while the woman had eaten hungrily, she had sat beside her opened trunks, still unable to believe the destruction her own brother had wrought. How he must hate her! There was no other explanation. He hated her!

Books she had treasured had been torn in two, pages defiled, scrawled upon in Felipe's childish hand. She had no clothes to wear, no shoes. Only one pair of riding boots which he had for some reason not damaged and the shoes she had worn the night Ruy came for her. Every shift she possessed had been mutilated too and her stockings and her beloved riding trousers. He knew he would hurt her by doing that and he had. Tears spilled silently down over her cheeks until Serafina could stand it no longer and knelt at her side, gathering her into her arms.

'Don't cry. That's what he wants, the devil. You have to fight him.'

'How? I don't know how,' she whispered, distraught.

'You have a man now.'

Instantly she drew back, brushing away the tears.

'No. I have no man. I have a husband who does not want me. I am as alone as I ever was. I am tired,

I am going to bed. Tomorrow I will burn everything here. What use is any of it to me?'

When she went downstairs the next morning Ruy was half-way through breakfast. She turned away the plate of food Terecita thrust before her and asked for coffee only.

He looked across the table at her, said quietly.

'You will need more than that.'

'I am not hungry.'

'Would you like to ride? Juan and Manuela are sleeping in late this morning. Come with me. You used to enjoy it.'

'When I was young and foolish,' she flung back. He left the table stony-faced and she sat in a miserable silence until she heard him go out to his horse. She was close on his heels and he turned in surprise as she called from the verandah.

'Wait. Please wait. I will come.'

'Pedro, bring another horse for the señora.'

'I have nothing to wear.'

'Come as you are. You never used to worry what you looked like.' A compliment or an insult? Ysanne wondered as she hurried down the steps to join him.

He did not make her feel at ease with conversation, but as they rode away from the house, up the slopes into the forest of pine and firs and the slender, gracious silver birch, Ysanne felt the tenseness within her slip away. She loved this country with every fibre of her being. She forgot his presence totally as she allowed her horse its head and it moved, slowly and with sure-footedness, over the rocky ground which led towards the mountain slopes. The air here was chilly, fresher than below. She shivered, but said nothing. The coldness sharpened her wits, made her realise what she had almost lost in her foolishness. She was mistress of Pinos Altos. This was her domain now as well as Ruy's. They would share it, work together for its welfare and the good of the *vaqueros* and their families, exactly as her father had once done at the ranch—as she had once wanted to do with Felipe.

Why had her brother wanted more? They had shared everything, or so she had thought, after she had returned home. A closeness they had not experienced for many years. Had she failed him in some way? She knew she had not. Felipe had gone his own way for reasons only he could explain. She wanted to know what they were, although she now knew she could never condone or forgive them!

'He is a fool,' she whispered to the tall trees about her. 'He has everything. Why does he want more?' And yet she knew the answer. He wanted perfection. He wanted Manuela.

'Take Manuela with you this afternoon.' She turned to Ruy, seized with a sudden feeling of apprehension.

'No . . . That is out of the question.'

'If Felipe comes for her at Pinos Altos, he will take her. I know it. Would you have her go through—through that?'

'Why are you so sure she is in danger?' Ruy caught the reins of her horse and brought her close to him. 'I have men enough to watch over you both.'

'He will not harm me. As you said, I am no longer of use to him. Manuela will give perfection to the strange world he lives in. Without her it is not complete. I cannot explain myself, I only know he will do anything to have her, no matter how foolhardy. Take her with you, please. I am frightened for her safety.'

Dismounting, Ruy lifted her down. Her loose hair brushed against his cheek and once again he was reminded of the night they had spent together. Three short days ago, it seemed more like years. An eternity. She broke free of his hold and began to walk quickly up the rocky path ahead of them, then stopped and sat down, gathering her skirts about her. Her cheeks were flushed with colour. Healthy colour, he thought as he cautiously joined her, expecting a rebuff at his closeness, but none came. She was a different person out there, he realised, free and uninhibited, untouched by the grief and pain of the past months.

He wanted to touch her, knew he dared not. He leaned back on one elbow, considering her with a directness of gaze she found so unnerving, she deliberately avoided it, concentrating her attention instead on the house and out-buildings spread out below them.

'Felipe could avoid your guards,' she insisted. 'If he does he will have clear access to the house. You came to the ranch and took me. Why should he not do the same with Manuela? His patrol in the valley may see you, but if Manuela was hidden in the wagon, he would think she was still here.'

'And he would find you instead. What do you think he would do then?'

'To me? His sister? Nothing. It is Manuela he wants. I have never meant anything to him, I realise that now. I was a pawn for Sancho. Everything that has happened has been a means to an end—his obtaining the thing he covets most. I will be safe here—or are you afraid I will run away while you are gone? You may have married me in order to keep your word to my father, Ruy, but don't tell me the valley never entered into it. Did you not think you would be able to manipulate me? Make me sign it over to your son perhaps, if not to you? That will never happen. It will be my daughter's inheritance. No one else's.'

'I have not spoken of the valley, have I?'

'I have not forgotten either, should I die before I have a daughter, it now goes to you. Tell me that is not what you want?'

'I have always maintained it should have passed to the male heirs. Look at the mess you are in now, a female owning land and not being able to protect it. Who is out there now? My men, not you, Ysanne.'

'That is unfair.'

'So is war which is just what your brother has declared. He has ordered no quarter too, if you remember!'

'Which is why you must take her with you. If he comes here many men will be killed defending her,' Ysanne insisted.

'*Sí*, and I do not want more of my people killed. I will take her with us,' Ruy replied with a nod. 'Why don't you come too and choose some new clothes.'

'I—no. I don't feel up to facing people yet. There would be too many questions.'

'You will have to show yourself if there is a trial,' she was reminded.

'That will be soon enough,' Ysanne said. 'Manuela can bring me back a few things.'

'As you wish. It's almost lunchtime. We must go back,' Ruy rose to his feet as if he was suddenly ill at ease in her company and she regretfully followed him back to the horses.

Manuela was overjoyed to be going into the town with Juan. She tried to persuade Ysanne to go with them also, but the other girl stayed adamant in her decision to remain behind.

'I shall be leaving Chato here, and some of the villagers who lost their homes in the valley have encamped nearer the house until we return. There are more than enough men to repel anyone from outside,' Ruy told Ysanne as they stood together on the verandah. Juan had been lifted into the wagon and Manuela was fussing over him, tucking blankets around him, fashioning one into a pillow for his head until he said with a grimace.

'Enough! I'm not an invalid. Get down here beside me and keep down as soon as we reach the lower trail. Don't even show yourself once until we are well on the other side of the valley.'

'To guard Pinos Altos or me?' Ysanne asked.

'I am not frightened you will leave, Ysanne,' Ruy said grimly. 'Where will you go? Back to a brother who has no further use for you? I don't think so? That aunt in Monterey? You are of no use to her either now you are married.'

'Anywhere would be preferable to here,' she flung back, but she did not mean the words.

He stared at her angrily as he pulled on a pair of black leather gloves.

'When I get back I shall expect my wife to be waiting for me. My wife, Ysanne, do you understand? If you are not prepared to be that, then you may as well leave today. Who knows, you may have your wish. A daughter to inherit the Valle de Lágrimas. *Dios*, what a little firebrand a daughter of ours would turn out to be, eh?'

'Is that a threat, Ruy?'

'An ultimatum. The choice is yours. Here's something else to think about while I am gone.'

Before she could guess his intentions, he had seized her in his arms and soundly kissed her, much to the delight of Manuela and Juan. His mouth on hers was not gentle and her lips felt bruised as he released her and strode to his horse. He was trying to force her hand. Unknowingly he had. She would be waiting for him when he returned. She would be his wife. In time perhaps, he might accept she really loved him, believe why she had gone away. Her wish would be answered one day. A daughter and if God willed it, a son. Every man wanted a son.

The house was very quiet after the noise of the wagon and horses had died away. Chato watched the cavalcade until it was out of sight, then began organising armed groups of men, despatching them to different places around the house and on the approach trail. He did not speak to her. She felt unwanted and useless watching him and eventually went inside and up to her room.

Serafina had unpacked the two trunks containing her useless clothes, and piled them all on to the bed.

'Look, *mi niña*, two undershifts he missed and a blouse. How that came to be in the wrong drawer, I do not know. It was wrapped around this.'

She was holding out a leather-bound book. No, not a book, Ysanne saw as she took it mystified. A diary!

'Papa's diary. He was always writing in this, do you remember?'

'Ever since you began to assume some responsibility for the ranch. He wrote in it most days and often while you were away.'

'He must have hidden it in my clothes. Why? What does it contain that he wants me to see?' Ysanne breathed. 'I am going to read it from cover to cover. Perhaps I might find the answers to my questions in here. There's a piece of paper too, Serafina,' her voice trailed off and she was silent, staring down at the paper in her hands.

'What is it? You look so strange?'

'Papa told me he would make a new will. This is it, revoking all others. He left the Hacienda de las Flores to me, not Felipe! It—it was witnessed by Pedro Valdez!'

'Not to your brother? But why was it hidden for you to find now?'

'Perhaps it wasn't. Perhaps Papa was hiding them both from Felipe. If he had discovered this, heavens knows what he would have done. I wonder if this is what the quarrel was about that day in the study. Ruy had come to the house knowing my father expected him to agree to the match between us. I know he told him about the new will. What if Felipe overheard and flew into one of his rages, struck Papa and then turned on Ruy. He would have had nothing, don't you see? No ranch, no Manuela. I would have everything I had ever wanted—and more.'

Trembling, Ysanne sank down into a chair and opened the diary. Written here would be her father's deepest thoughts, his fears and hopes. For her there would be answers. Some she would not like perhaps, but she had to read it!

CHAPTER TEN

CURLED up in a comfortable chair in her bedroom at Pinos Altos, Ysanne allowed nothing to disturb her concentration as she read her father's diary. It was all there. Every detail that had ever needed an explanation. Every answer to her questions. It was not pleasant, but it could not be discarded. She knew, distasteful as it would be, and painful, the book would have to be handed to Sancho. He would have to decide, after reading it, whether Felipe should go to trial or not. He would, of course. The facts described on the pages open before her would have many witnesses willing to testify to their authenticity. Friends and enemies alike, she thought ruefully.

Serafina placed a tray of coffee and cakes on the table before her. She allowed herself the luxury of a hot cup of reviving coffee and a little food. She had been reading for over four hours. It would be dark soon. She was glad she had not bundled her clothes into a heap and had them burned, as had been her first intention when she saw them. The diary and the will would have been lost. Felipe might have gone on ruining the peace of the valley, killing without one iota of conscience, using people useful to him to gain his own ends.

Manuela would never belong to him now. She was safe in the town with Juan and Ruy. Ysanne was glad she had insisted on the girl going too. Now, more than ever, she realised how cruel her brother could be, to what lengths he would go. It was unbelievable, yet the proof lay in her hands. Her father would not have written lies, knowing she might some day read them. Truth! The truth she had refused to acknowledge since the day he had died. She had been blind, but now her eyes were open!

'Serafina . . .' Her voice trembled with emotion. 'Did—did you know what this contained?'

'Me? Do I read your father's most treasured thoughts? What do you think I am? They were meant for only two people—you and him.'

'Why not Felipe?' she queried. 'Did he not prove invaluable when Papa was ill? You told me yourself how he took over the running of the *hacienda*. Are you telling me different now?'

Serafina muttered something quite unintelligible under her breath and crossed herself.

'What do you want me to tell you? How I watched Don Diego eating his heart out until the day you returned? It was not your fault his health deteriorated. It was not your fault he did not write and tell you at once how ill he was. It was not your fault that when he did the letter was prevented from leaving the house. That and others he wrote afterwards, imploring you to come home and marry the man of your choice, the man he had arranged a match with. He was so sure Don Ruy would accept his offer.'

'What did he offer him?' Ysanne asked in a hollow tone.

'You! Just you. He was right, I listen at keyholes. That way I know what is going on and I do not have to believe the half-truths or the lies I am told. He did not give your secret away. At first, I know, the señor did not believe what he was told, but your father was most persuasive. You must have loved this *hombre* very much for him to be so persistent.'

'He did not agree,' Ysanne cried. 'On the way home that day he told me he had not made up his mind.'

'Rubbish!' Serafina's nose wrinkled in disgust. There was nothing she did not know, as her mistress would soon discover. 'After you had gone upstairs to change, Don Felipe also left the room. The moment he did so, your father and Ruy Valdez concluded the marriage arrangements—and he told him of the very generous dowry he would have on your wedding day. I heard a promise too—a promise that Don Ruy would take care of you! No matter what the circumstances. Your father was most emphatic on that point. This *hombre* must think something of you too, to give such a promise.'

'Then—then my father knew he was going to die?'

'Of course, and he faced it like a man, as he had faced everything else over the years.'

'Like Felipe. Acknowledging a son he knew was not his son because he still loved the wife who betrayed him. *Madre mía*, she did not know what harm she was doing. We are all paying for her moment of foolishness.'

Serafina's mouth sagged. Ysanne suddenly realised how, in her moment of need, she had given away the secret which Felipe did not know, but which ruled all their lives.

'Sit down. I will tell you why my father was so anxious for me to marry Ruy. *Sí*, I loved him. I still love him. What I feel cannot be destroyed by doubts. I thought once it could, but I was wrong. I belong to him. I am his wife. I will always be his wife. If he never loves me it will not matter so long as I am with him.'

'Not love you?' Serafina echoed. 'Do you think your beloved father would have given you into the keeping of a man who did not feel as you do? You went away too soon. On your birthday he was going to ask for your hand, *mi niña*. He thought you had left because you no longer loved your home, that his case was hopeless.'

Ysanne sat motionless in her chair. Could fate really have been so cruel? Was that why her father had planned to change his will? To give her a fine dowry to take to the man she loved on the most wonderful day in her life? That was only part of it, she realised. As always, he had been trying to protect her.

'You know so much, Serafina, but your knowledge only touched the surface of our troubles. In this diary my father has, as you thought, unburdened his soul. The legacy he has left is not one to rejoice at. As you know, both my father and mother were very conscious of their Spanish origins. My father more so, I think, like Sancho. Perhaps in those early days he was too strict, I don't know. All I know, from what he has written, is that my—my mother met someone else. Our neighbour, before Don Sancho bought the nearby *hacienda*. They became more than friends. Do you understand me?'

Serafina swallowed hard and nodded. She dared not put what she was thinking into words.

'Felipe is the result of that—friendship. My

mother kept the secret of her betrayal until the day she died, then the burden became too much for her and she told my father. He at once sought out the man, as was expected of him, but he found something he had not bargained for. Something that has been haunting him for many years. I think he knew of my mother's infidelity, but in his heart he forgave her because she had given him a son and that was important to him, but after her death, when he attempted to trace her lover, who had apparently moved to San Francisco after selling his *hacienda* to Sancho, he found . . .' Her voice trailed off into a miserable silence. 'His long search ended in a terrible place, Serafina. A home for the insane. Felipe's father, in his remaining years on earth, had become a madman. Two people—sometimes passive and normal, but at other times, a devious wild man. I have seen my brother's moods and now, I realise, I have seen his father in him. Poor Papa. The son he tried so hard to love was not only not his, but in his early life had begun to show signs of madness. He kept it from me, from his best friend Pedro Valdez, from Ruy, even though at times, I now know he must have hinted at it, from what Ruy has told me. Serafina, I had begun to think my blood was tainted, that I might some day share my brother's wild moods and cruelty. I have been spared . . . but he . . .'

'Oh, my poor love.' Serafina slid off her chair and wrapped her arms around Ysanne's shivering form. 'Don't read any more. I can only guess what it will tell you.'

'It is too late. I have finished it. I know of my father's suspicions—that Felipe waylaid and killed Pedro. He told Ruy. He told him so much without actually accusing anyone. He left it all up to Ruy to prove. That was all he could do, knowing he was going to die. He was so brave.'

'So is your husband, to take on such a task, *mi niña*. Have you thought of that? He could say so little to you when you come home. You say your father kept your secret, so he thought you had left a sick old man alone. I know, I heard him, but he still wanted you.'

He wanted her! She had been his wife for one night only, but he still wanted her! He had issued an ultimatum—'Be here when I return and be my wife, or get out, back to a brother who does not want you'. She would not be waiting. She would go after him to the town, taking with her the diary and the new will. He must see them, and know by her bringing them to him that there must be no further dissent between them, that she knew he wanted her. She dared not think of love. Not yet. Perhaps that would come. Now, all that mattered was that he had cared for her enough to ask her father for her hand in marriage. It was a starting point. After that anything was possible.

So much had happened. So much that had threatened to part them, tried to destroy her love. It had not happened. She would ask Chato to take her to her husband. Serafina looked at her in surprise.

'Him! You trust him?'

Sí. Because of the love I know he has for my husband.'

'He will kill you and leave you in the valley. Think how convenient it would be. Who would believe he had done it after the things that have been happening?'

'Please, Serafina, I know what I have to do. Will you ask Chato to come up here now?'

Reluctantly the woman went away. She did not agree with what her mistress was about to do, but then she rarely did. When Chato arrived, she stood close to Ysanne's chair protectively.

'I want you to escort me into the town. It is very important,' Ysanne said, looking into the hostile face before her.

'That is impossible, señora. I am needed here, nor can I delegate the task to anyone else. We need every man here. Beside, Don Ruy will be back tomorrow.'

Ysanne rose determinedly to her feet.

'I am going with or without you. I have the proof Don Ruy needs to convince the courts of my brother's guilt.' She held the book out for him to see. 'Take it. Look at it. My father's diary and a new will which you can see leaves the *hacienda* to me, not Felipe. I must get this to him before my brother does something else to harm innocent people.'

In silence the man flicked through several pages and she saw his mouth tighten.

'We shall have to ride swiftly. It is getting late. We will have to risk going through the Valle de Lágrimas. Are you prepared for that?'

'*Sí.*' There was no hesitation in Ysanne's answer.

'You love him,' Chato said.

'You do not believe me—or is it just that you disapprove?'

'Who am I to say what should be. I always knew you would be the one for him, but a wild stallion must have its head. You will never tame him. No more will he tame you,' the indian remarked calmly. 'You are both beasts of the forest. You will claw at each other, inflict pain, and yet remain faithful to each other until the day you die. I saw that a long time ago. Even after you had come back and there was bitterness between you, I told him how it would be. He was a fool to have waited for so long.'

'If I had stayed, do you mean it might have been different?' Perhaps her father would still be alive. Pedro too. No trouble in the valley. 'You are very cruel. I could not have stopped what has happened.'

'Life is cruel. Very well. I will have two horses saddled. We leave as soon as you are ready, señora.' He still did not approve of her, Ysanne thought as she hurried to Manuela's room and found herself a warm blouse and a woollen cloak, but he dared not refuse to take her now he knew how important the journey was.

He gave a nod of approval as he saw she had prepared well for the ride, helped her to mount and motioned her to follow close behind him as he started down the trail towards low ground. Serafina stood watching them out of sight, still convinced, Ysanne suspected, that she would never see her mistress again.

Within ten minutes of leaving the house, Ysanne noticed an alertness about her companion that made her feel uneasy. He slowed the pace of his horse and she did likewise, closing with him to ask worriedly,

'What is it?'

'Something is wrong.' Chato's eyes swept the trees and bushes around them. In the swiftly gathering dusk she could see nothing, hear nothing unusual, then suddenly she realised how silent the forest was. No birds singing as they always did until well after sunset, no movement of animals scurrying for cover as their horses approached. 'There are strangers about. Stay here and don't move until I come back.'

She did not disobey the order. His instincts were sharper than hers, his movements far more stealthy than hers would have been as he slipped to the ground and disappeared into the shadowy foliage ahead of them. Still no movement, not a sound as he moved away from her. She shivered as the only logical explanation for the strange lack of activity struck her. Felipe! Surely not? He would bring many men with him, hoping to storm the house. Sancho himself had said he had been trying to rouse support among his friends, few that they were these days. Or would he? His cunning mind had already devised many schemes she had thought incredible and impossible. What if he came alone to pluck Manuela from Pinos Altos? One man might possibly slip past the sentries, into the house. What if he had watched Ruy and the others leave and seen an unexpected chance to have the girl he desired? In his madness, might he not think himself invincible against all odds?

'Chato, let us go on,' she ordered in a quiet tone.

'You are a great disappointment to me, little sister.' Felipe's voice. She froze in terror. 'Don't move or this *indio* friend of yours will have a large hole in his head.'

The words were accompanied by an amused chuckle. It was an awful sound. Chato stumbled out of the undergrowth, with Felipe on his heels, a pistol menacing his back. The indian's face bore no expression, even though, as they drew closer, she could see blood trickling from a gash on his forehead. Her brother's eyes gleamed with mockery as they regarded her.

'I believe congratulations are in order, Señora Valdez. Are you his wife? No last-minute doubts when he took you in his arms? No, I can see by your face you did not, you treacherous bitch! Soon, very soon, you will be a widow.'

'Felipe, it is madness for you to be here.' What was she saying? He was mad and it was now obvious to her she had been right in her assumption he cared little for his own skin. 'Ruy has men everywhere. The house is surrounded. He knows everything, even about the men you have had here working for you. That is why he has gone into the town. To bring back the sheriff and Sancho. Go quickly, before they return and you are caught.'

'Knows? He may suspect, but he knows nothing. A little accident may happen to his unfortunate prisoners before he returns and then what proof will he have? It will be my word against his. He will come to the ranch hoping to take back Manuela and I shall have men waiting for him.' Felipe gloated in what he thought was a moment of triumph. He had slipped past two guards while the fools were enjoying a few minutes' relaxation, smoking. The third man he had encountered had died beneath his knife blade without knowing the identity of his assailant.

'Manuela?' Ysanne echoed, 'but she . . .' A warning look from Chato silenced her.

'Is back at Pinos Altos waiting for me to collect her. I told her I would the other day, but she was afraid Juan would stop me. I stopped him instead, didn't I?'

'*Sí*, Felipe, you did that. You—you are going to take her with you then?' She had to play for time. Perhaps someone else would be as suspicious as Chato and come to investigate, or they would be seen as they approached the house. Mad he might be, but not stupid. He would not openly ride up to Pinos Altos with them as his prisoners. When he discovered Manuela was not at home . . . She thrust that thought from her mind.

'And you. That way I shall be doubly sure Ruy will come after me. When he is dead there will be no one to keep Manuela and I apart and Sancho can have you with my blessing. The old fool still wants you, I knew it by the way he spoke when he came to tell me you were married. You really should not have gone against me in this manner, Ysanne. I am very displeased with you.'

There was nothing in his manner or in his tone to tell her the madness which had been inside him since childhood was beginning to master him completely, but she knew it instinctively. Knew also that her life and that of anyone who got in his way again, was in danger. Could she humour him? Would he believe a show of sisterly love?

'Mount up behind her, *indio*, and remember, if you flicker so much as an eyelid, I shall put a bullet through her head. Not yours—hers!'

'Felipe, how you over-dramatise,' she returned, mocking indignation. 'I am sorry I have offended you by marrying against your wishes, but as you have always been so sure of what you wanted and allowed nothing to stand in your way, as your sister, I thought it a compliment to your steadfastness that I followed suit. Surely you can forgive me.' Chato climbed up behind her. His body against hers was tense, showing his displeasure for what he thought to be a betrayal of his *amigo*, Ruy. As Felipe caught up the reins of the spare horse, she half-turned, slipped the diary she had taken from her pocket into the man's hands. 'Get this to safety if you can,' she whispered. 'Do not fear for me. I will bluff him as long as I can.'

Chato sat behind her like a statue, his lips hardly moved as he spoke.

'He will kill you.' The eyes which regarded her were no longer cold and suspicious, they held a silent acknowledgement of what she was trying to do—and respect, something she had never received from him before.

'Think of yourself and what you carry, not me,' she insisted. 'As soon as you have an advantage over him, take it.'

'You said something, Ysanne?' Felipe was watching her with narrowed gaze.

'I thought I heard a noise.'

'Hoping are you? The only guard near us is dead, my dear. Ride beside me. Don't attempt to break away. To the house. To Manuela,' he ordered.

'I have told you there are men there. They will kill you. What will Manuela do then, Felipe?'

'Kill me? When I have a pistol at the head of the wife of Ruy Valdez? It is more than their worthless lives to open fire when you might be hit. If they did not kill you, I most certainly would.'

'You would kill me? Your own sister?'

He smiled and she quickly looked away.

'You don't understand, do you? You never have. Until I have what I want I will use any methods, stop at nothing. Anyone in my way will be killed. The sooner you accept that, the better. Accept it and help me take Manuela back to the house and I shall allow you to marry Sancho, after a suitable period of mourning for your dear departed husband, of course, and raise your children in peace and harmony. I shall expect you to sign over the Valle de Lágrimas to me before you remarry and to give up any designs you have on the ranch itself. I once told you, what is mine, I keep. I share with no one. Ride on.'

You do not own our home, she almost said, but stopped herself in time. Anyone in my way will be killed he had said, as he killed Pedro Valdez, perhaps his own father and attempted to kill Juan. Biting her lips fiercely to keep back a rush of tears to her eyes, she began to ride slowly back the way she had come.

Rifles came up to menace them as they approached the house, then were lowered as Chato called urgently,

'Not one shot is to be fired. Do you not see who he holds hostage?' Several of the men were slow in doing so. Men from the village which had been burned the day she came home, Ysanne saw, inwardly trembling. Without hesitation Felipe shot the man nearest to him, and ordered Ysanne,

'Dismount and stand by my horse.'

She had no choice but to obey. No one dared make a move to approach the shot man who lay unmoving on the ground. Another victim of her brother's madness. She was seized with an impulse to throw herself at his gun arm, give Chato a chance to leap from the horse. The look Felipe directed at her told her he knew her thoughts—and she knew the outcome of such a foolish attempt at bravery.

Chato slid from the saddle to join her, touched

her arm and shook his head as she looked enquiringly into his bronzed features.

'Wise,' Felipe drawled. 'Into the house both of you. Manuela and I long to be together again. How she misses me each time we are parted. This is the last time. *Dios mío*, I have waited so long for this night.'

On feet of lead, Ysanne led the way into the house. A startled Terecita, coming out of the kitchen with a tray of wine glasses for the dining-room, began to speak, saw Felipe and the weapon trained on Ysanne and promptly dropped the tray at her feet. The noise brought Serafina out of the bedroom. She took one look at the scene below and started down the stairs, coming straight for Felipe, her eyes blazing, ignoring the weapon which turned in her direction.

'No,' Ysanne screamed and flung herself at her brother. At the same time Chato hurled himself at Felipe, knocking him to the floor, but he did not lose his grip on the pistol. It came up to menace the indian as he bent over his fallen opponent, intent on finishing what he had started.

There came the sound of a second shot and Chato reeled backwards, clutching his face. The bullet had sliced one cheek and it was pouring with blood.

'Where is Manuela? Bring her to me.' Felipe was on his feet again. She expected anger, but he was calm and that frightened her as much as one of his rages.

'She—she has gone riding,' she stammered.

'In the dark?'

'She left the same time as we did. She cannot have gone far. She is worried, Felipe, she needs to be alone. Did—did she say what time she would be back, Serafina?'

'No,' it was Terecita who answered. 'But I expect her for dinner. I have cooked venison. It is her favourite. She will not be late.'

'Fetch some water and a cloth,' Ysanne instructed. 'We will be in the *sala*.' Without waiting for her brother's approval, she took Chato's arm and helped him into the room. Felipe followed, his pistol still aimed in Ysanne's direction as she did what little she could to stem the flow of blood and clean the wound. Serafina hovered at her side and the look in her eyes proclaimed she was no longer afraid of Felipe. She hated him for destroying what few personal belongings she possessed, as he had done with his own sister. And Chato hated him for killing his son, Ysanne thought, as she looked from one hostile face to the other. They had to do something before Felipe began to grow suspicious at Manuela's continued absence, but what? One of them would surely be injured or killed if they attempted to rush him, but what other choice did they have?

'Take this away and bring some hot coffee,' Ysanne instructed Terecita.

'Be quick about it and return alone, woman, or I shall kill them all and then you,' Felipe snapped as she hurriedly headed towards the door.

'If you kill me you will never leave Pinos Altos alive,' Ysanne told him calmly, and he turned to consider her slowly, his gaze wandering for a long moment over her borrowed attire.

'Did you receive your clothes safely and all your precious little bits and pieces.' He laughed at the pun.

'That was very cruel of you.'

'What did you expect? I found it a most satisfying experience. Moments like that have been rare in my life. Apart from the time I despatched our dear father to his eternal rest, I can't remember another so exhilarating. Ruy's death may outdo them both, of course, especially as you are going to watch me kill him. It will be a lesson to you not to try and upset my plans again.'

'Ruy—Ruy spoke the truth.' Ysanne's voice was barely audible as she stepped towards him, fists clenching. 'You struck him in the study.'

'And held a pillow over his foolish mouth until he breathed his last. Did you think I would let a feeble old man stand in my way, any more than I shall tolerate your stubbornness, my dear sister? He tried to tell me I was the son of a madman, not of his blood. I could not allow him to tell everyone such a lie, could I?'

The pistol was between them, his hand was steady and she saw his finger tighten around the trigger as she moved even closer. She did not care if he fired, or if she was killed. He had to be stopped!

'You have lost, Felipe. Everything you want! Manuela, the valley, the ranch. Shall I tell you and put you out of your misery? Papa made a new will. You always suspected, I think, but you never knew for sure. Well, he did and I found it, together with the diary he hid in some of my clothes. You left me a few things undamaged, Felipe, you were careless in your moment of destruction. Perhaps if you had not been enjoying yourself so much, you would have noticed them.' Out of the corner of her eye, she became aware of Chato edging to one side of her brother whose full attention was centred on her.

'The diary contained Papa's fears about you. The new will he made, witnessed by Pedro Valdez, another kindly old man you also murdered, leaves everything to me. Everything, Felipe. As for Manuela, she is not here. She went with Juan and Ruy into the town. I gave Ruy both items before he left to give to the sheriff.'

'Not here?' Felipe's eyes glazed for a moment as if he had difficulty in comprehending her words and then they were wide and staring and she was afraid again. 'She has gone riding, you said.'

'I persuaded Ruy to take her away from here, to safety. You will never have her. He will protect her against you as father tried to, as Pedro tried. He will succeed. They will not be back here for days.'

'Liar!' He screamed the word at her and his clenched fist struck her across the face, sending her crashing backwards into a chair where she lay half-stunned. As Serafina started towards her, he fired and she crumpled to the floor almost at Ysanne's feet. She heard herself begin to scream hysterically, then, as Chato hurled himself forward, she cried,

'Don't. He'll kill you. He's mad! Do you hear me? Mad!'

A great blackness threatened to descend over her. Fighting it off, she struggled to her feet, knelt at Serafina's side. Her left shoulder was covered in blood, but she was still breathing.

'Thank God,' Ysanne breathed. She stumbled to her feet again, wheeling around to face her brother.

He stood facing Chato and she knew he was going to pull the trigger again, but the Navajo seemed unconcerned, then as he spoke she realised why.

'One more barrel, señor. That is all you have.' And she realised for the first time the weapon Felipe held was a 'pepperbox' with four barrels. He had used one on the man outside, one on Chato, the third on Serafina. Her eyes scanned the room for a heavy object, knowing it was Chato's intention to sacrifice himself in the hope she could somehow overcome him. The heavy statue on the sideboard carved of pine. A perfect weapon. If only she could reach it, hurl it at her brother before he took another life.

'Then I must decide.' Felipe's tone was flat, emotionless, not so the eyes which looked from one to the other. 'Who is the most dangerous, I wonder? You, *indio*? What can you do to me? On the other hand, you, my sister know too much. Mad, am I? Then you share my madness for we had the same parents.'

'No, you did not,' a voice declared behind him. Ysanne raised her eyes to the doorway, unbelieving of the figures she saw clustered there. Sancho, a pistol levelled at Felipe's back, several *vaqueros* from outside, Juan leaning heavily against the door jamb—and Ruy, stepping into the room. Not behind her brother to attack him from a position of advantage, but to one side of him, in clear view. 'Diego was not your real father. He is still alive—and completely mad.'

'You knew?' Ysanne asked faintly. 'All this time and not a word to me?'

'I tried to spare your feelings. In the beginning you would not have believed me and afterwards, it did not matter. I acted as I thought best. Think of me what you will, Ysanne, it was for the best. In a few short hours, the day you returned home, I came to claim a bride, discovered the truth of Felipe's birth and was accused of attempted murder.'

It was no wonder he had looked as he had when he left the house, she realised, ashamed. For her sake he had remained silent, tried to fight Felipe alone, not even confiding in his own brother, or Sancho, who could have helped him. She knew by the latter's presence, the truth had at last been revealed.

'Where is Manuela? I want Manuela,' Felipe insisted, oblivious to the determined faces surrounding him. Ysanne doubted if he even saw them. He was looking for only one. 'Why do you say I am mad? Father said so too, that is why I had to kill him.'

'Somewhere where you will never touch her,' Sancho replied grimly. 'Put aside your pistol, Felipe, perhaps I can help you. Believe me, you do need it.'

'Help me? Why should I need help?' Felipe's expression became quite surprised. 'I have come for my bride. Don't keep her from me. Let me see her.'

Dear heaven, Ysanne thought, he does not even remember what he has done. Despite Ruy's warning hand, she stepped towards him.

'Felipe, listen to him. There are doctors who can help you. I promise I will not let anyone harm you. Come, give me your pistol.'

'Will you take me to Manuela? Everything I have done has been only for her.'

'I will try,' she promised. She would promise anything to stop anyone else being hurt.

'No, you won't! You are lying, like them. You want to kill me too.' He sprang back from her, the pistol waving erratically from Ruy to Chato and then her and back again to Ruy.

'He cannot kill us all,' Ruy said in a low tone. 'Take him.'

Felipe watched the figures slowly converging on him. The terror registering in his eyes was like that of a trapped animal. Frantically Ysanne waved them back.

'I had to kill them, little sister. You know that, don't you? They did not want me to have her and that was not right. We love each other, you see. You know that too, don't you?'

'Felipe. Oh, Felipe.' Tears choked back the words she knew he wanted to hear. Tears for the brother she had never known, and yet also for the one she had, but in whose closed world she had never shared anything. A strange, almost peaceful expression settled over his features.

'Bring her to me,' he ordered quietly. 'It is time we were leaving.'

'I will fetch her. She is packing now,' Ysanne lied, with wildly beating heart, then her voice broke and huge sobs racked her shoulders.

The cry Felipe uttered made Ysanne smother her ears with her hands. It was the agonised cry of a man whose world had just been destroyed. In that final moment, as he placed the muzzle of the pepperpot against his mouth and fired, she knew her lie had not deceived him. Knew he was sane. Sane enough for one moment, time enough to destroy the demon within him—and himself.

Ruy tried to hold her back, but she slipped to her knees beside him. Felipe died as she did so, the smile still lingering on his face.

'Ysanne, my dear, I am so sorry, but it is better for him it ended this way. You were very kind to him. It gave him peace before he died.' Sancho was beside her, gently drawing her away.

She stared at him, dull-eyed, her senses numb with shock. Chato moved forward and held out the book she had given him. She wanted to laugh aloud as she saw it. What use was it now? Felipe was dead.

'Take this. Read it, but please, never reveal its contents to an outsider. It is all the proof you need, but you cannot convict a dead man,' she pleaded. 'Let him rest in peace. I ask this for him, not me.'

'After what he did to you? Would have done to you had he lived?' Ruy asked quietly. She was aware of the men coming and going from the room, helping Chato outside, carrying Serafina upstairs.

'I must go to her,' she said, but Sancho's restraining hand was on her arm.

'What is this piece of paper?'

'Papa's new will, properly witnessed as you will see. He left everything to me,' she answered, still watching the unconscious form of her maid being carried to her room. 'Please send for a doctor someone . . .'

'I already have,' Ruy assured her. She was so deathly pale he thought she was going to faint. It was over, but what was left, if anything? Chato had told him she was coming to him, complete with the proof he wanted. That was when Felipe had been alive, bent on more destruction. His death could be the last remaining thing to part them for ever. She looked so fragile, more vulnerable than he had ever thought possible. 'It's over, Ysanne. The Valle de Lágrimas is at peace once more.

'Stay with us tonight, Sancho,' he said. 'We have both ridden far and hard today. I thank God you decided to come here instead of waiting for us to come to you. If we had been forced to go all the way to town, instead of meeting you half-way, we would never have come back here in time.' He looked at Ysanne and gradually beneath his intense gaze, colour began to return to her cheeks as she remembered the ultimatum he had issued to her before he left. 'If you wish, Sancho can take you home in the morning.'

'I am home,' she whispered. She looked at him shocked. Did he want her to go?

Sancho gave some excuse that he wanted to have an early night in order to study the diary before he left, gave her a gentle, almost fatherly kiss on the cheek and left the room. Everyone had gone Ysanne realised, as she looked around her.

'You are staying?' Ruy asked. How she wished he would take her in his arms and give her the comfort she so desperately needed.

'If—if you want me.'

'Want you? In heaven's name, girl, you are all I have ever wanted. If you had not been such a stubborn, disbelieving little wildcat, it might have been possible for me to tell you long ago,' he replied.

'Tell me now,' Ysanne whispered.

'Now I can tell you what took place that day in your father's study. Before, it was impossible.' His arm went around her waist, drawing her trembling body against his. 'When I told you I had not committed myself to marriage, that was not the truth, but there were many things to be settled before I allowed myself to tell you of my feelings, or allowed Diego to spring on you the surprise arrangements for our marriage that he had been making ever since you went away. I thought you had left home because you had grown bored with the life here and when I came to Monterey to see you and watched you being fawned over by those young *caballeros*, saw you in the street or at the theatre in your fine clothes, I was plagued by more doubts. You seemed so happy, so much at ease.'

'Every moment I was looking forward to the day I came home,' Ysanne whispered. 'Of you, never of any other man!'

'I was a fool, I admit it! I even told Diego it was not right to continue with the arrangements, but he was adamant. He knew what I did not, of course. When you left us alone that day he told me he would announce our engagement at your homecoming party . . .'

'And I would have worn my white dress. I had it made to dazzle you,' she interrupted as he buried his lips against her hair. 'Go on. What else did Papa tell you? How did the quarrel start?'

'He showed me a copy of the new will he had made. He intended to tell you and everyone else about that at the party too. I advised him against it, thinking of Felipe's reaction, but he did not seem to be interested in that. Only you—and me. And then he said a strange, a frightening thing, "Felipe is not of my blood. His real father lies incurably insane in some asylum in San Francisco." He gave me no details. It was then he made me promise I would marry you quickly. He was afraid for your safety. There is more. I have kept all these things locked in my heart, Ysanne, told them to no one, not even Juan. On our wedding day, possession of the waterhole passed to me, although I can no longer prove it. Felipe came in as your father was reading the document to me. He flew into a rage, grabbed it and tore it into tiny pieces and threw them in my face, threatening both his father and me.

'Your father slapped him and received in return a savage blow that knocked him to the ground. Felipe threw a chair at me as I went to help him and as I staggered to my feet, I saw him holding your father by the head and banging him repeatedly against the desk. I lost my temper. I don't deny it. I saw the look in his eyes, the same one Manuela told me she had seen as he moved towards Juan with a rock in his hands, and I knew the madness within him was growing stronger. There was no knowing how long it would be before he was like his father . . .'

'Don't,' Ysanne pleaded. 'I have seen the way he looked many times. His madness made him so cunning. At first it was easy to believe everything he told me. I sent you away when I should have listened to you . . .'

'You were in a state of shock. I was angry, too angry to stop and explain when you accused me of . . . Never mind, that's past. He must have seen you coming downstairs before I did, that's why he called out so convincingly, playing the part of an anguished son whose father had just been brutally attacked,' Ruy said, his arms tightening around her.

'Poor Felipe.'

'It's over, *mi vida*. We must put it behind us and think of the future. Our future.'

Mi vida! My life! Simple words spoken from the heart which told her the depths of his love. For a moment she relaxed against him, gaining strength from his solidness. Her cheek resting against his shoulder, he watched the shadows of fear and doubt slowly disappearing from her eyes. Then, as he tilted back her head and kissed her with sudden, possessive passion, her hands crept up to lock around his neck, and her lips, fired to a response he had never felt before, confirmed what she had already told him, what he had not dared hope was true. And gave promise of a golden future he had thought forbidden to them both.

A very special gift for Mother's Day

You love Mills & Boon romances. Your mother will love this attractive Mother's Day gift pack. First time in paperback, four superb romances by leading authors. A very special gift for Mother's Day.

United Kingdom £4.40   On sale from 24th Feb 1984

A Grand Illusion
Maura McGiveny

Sensual Encounter
Carole Mortimer

Desire in the Desert
Mary Lyons

Aquamarine
Madeleine Ker

Look for this gift pack where you buy Mills & Boon romances.

Mills & Boon